"I want my ranch back."

"Enough to let me stay on peacefully?" Zoe asked in reply.

"Why the hell should I?" J.D. demanded. His voice went low, to an almost intimate growl. "Why should I do you any favors?"

Sensuality was so thick between them suddenly that the air was hard to breathe. Zoe's voice was barely above a whisper as she acknowledged, "I guess from your point of view there's no reason. I don't want to take over. I don't want anything more than for you to honor the fact that we have a legal paper giving me the right to live here. Can we get along peacefully?"

"That remains to be seen...."

Dear Reader,

Harlequin Romance would like to welcome you back to the ranch again with our yearlong miniseries, **HITCHED!** We've rounded up twelve of our most popular authors, and the result is a whole year of romance Western-style: cool cowboys, rugged ranchers and, of course, the women who tame them.

Look out in December for:

A Mistletoe Marriage
by
Jeanne Allan

Happy Reading, partners!

The Editors
Harlequin Romance

How the West was wooed!

The Cowboy
Wants a Wife!
Susan Fox

Harlequin Books

TORONTO • NEW YORK • LONDON
AMSTERDAM • PARIS • SYDNEY • HAMBURG
STOCKHOLM • ATHENS • TOKYO • MILAN
MADRID • WARSAW • BUDAPEST • AUCKLAND

ISBN 0-373-03432-6

THE COWBOY WANTS A WIFE!

First North American Publication 1996.

Copyright © 1996 by Susan Fox.

CHAPTER ONE

JOHN Dalton Hayes reined in his sorrel gelding at the edge of the pecan trees that formed the east boundary of the two acre lawn surrounding the main house on the Hayes Ranch. His ranch, passed down to him through five generations of Hayes fathers and sons, his home. He knew every rock of it, every blade of Texas grass. He'd ruled over its thirty thousand acres with the considerable force of his strong will like a benevolent despot: benevolent when he could afford to be, despot the other ninety-five percent of the time. He'd poured his sweat and blood into his ranch like the hard, uncompromising men before him, and wrested a living and a life-style from the obstinate ground just as they had. No threat, either man-made or of nature, had ever been able to shake a Hayes man's iron grip of possession. Until now.

Anger at himself and the world in general churned in his gut. The shameful knowledge that the threat to the Hayes Ranch in his generation had been a blonde cocktail waitress with movie star aspirations crawled around his insides every waking moment and haunted many a sleepless night.

He'd lost his head to Raylene Shannon on one of his few trips to Dallas for a rare bit of hell-raising. And raised hell they had, for three nights in his motel room until his guilty conscience prodded him into showing her the respect of a marriage proposal. After the quickie wedding, the hell-raising continued, but this time, it was the hell-raising year of being leg-shackled to a woman who hated his home and hated him because he couldn't understand her aspirations for stardom. His reluctance to invest mega bucks to ensure her rise to fame sent the flames higher, burning off any promise of real love, leaving them both with the cold ashes of regret.

Then came the most tortuous kind of hell-raising. The hell of losing a chunk of capital and a third of his ranch in the divorce. Money could be replenished by sweat and know-how. Getting Raylene to let him pay market price to buy back that third of his ranch had been impossible—her revenge for delaying by a year her star billing on the silver screen.

And now she'd sold that one-third interest to some Hollywood loonie. He'd refused to attend the meeting of his lawyer with his new co-owner and her lawyer. Refused to extend the courtesy of meeting the woman, but sending with his lawyer an offer to buy her out at a brow-raising profit. Which she'd turned down.

And now it was the first of June and his new co-owner was due to arrive any moment to take up residence. His lawyer had glossed over personal information about the mystery woman, but he'd been annoyingly specific when he warned J.D. about her rights and his obligations. All he had to go on was that she was a glamorous blue-eyed blonde, and that she'd signed every legal document with a godawful name that he took as both a portent of doom and a sure indication of ditzy character: Zoe Yahzoo.

As he rounded the front corner of the lawn, a movement drew his attention toward the ranch drive. A slim woman strolled along the whitewashed fence toward a small cluster of cows and calves. A deep-crowned Stetson shaded her profile and he glimpsed a pair of large-lensed sunglasses. Dressed cowboy chic in black lizardskin boots, tight designer jeans and a bright blue

silk blouse, the woman was like an electric flash on his
vision. The huge silver buckle at her waist winked at him
when she turned to stroll back. The woman was petite,
her small size and feminine aura multiplied several times
over in contrast to the cattle on the other side of the
fence.

John Dalton Hayes was a man who knew few fears,
and was as stunned as he was ashamed of the faint twist
of fear in his gut. A strange uncertainty gripped him as
he watched the woman stop and reach between the rails
of the fence to coax a calf closer. The urge to ride off
to the harsh comfort of open spaces battled with the
more familiar urge to ride straight to the problem and
stare it down. In the end, the big man was aware of a
sort of compromise as he nudged the sorrel along the
front edge of the yard. When he reached the ranch drive
opposite her, he drew his horse to a halt and watched.

A brash red convertible, which the house had blocked
from his view, was parked under the trees that shaded
part of the driveway. The California license plates
cinched it, more grim reminders that his domain was
being invaded by a Hollywood socialite.

Grateful for the sunglasses, which would conceal the
intensity of his observation of his new "partner," J.D.
focused his attention on the woman. He needed to gauge
how much of an unfriendly welcome he could get by
with without overstepping the legal constrictions of the
joint tenancy. His lawyer's description of her as a glamorous blonde suggested a type of fragility that might
make her easy to intimidate.

His hope was for her to find an association with him
intolerable, but he didn't want to come off a bully. Since
she was from Hollywood, he figured any romance toward
the west that might have inspired her to come here would

get choked out by the day-to-day isolation and reality of ranch living. Hollywood was a dreamworld, and the people who lived that life probably didn't have enough encounters with reality to believe in it the first few times. He planned to discourage any delusional ideas on her part, hoped for her to detest living on a Texas ranch. Once that was accomplished, she'd sell out to him and hightail it back to fairyland ASAP. Then, challenge overcome, he'd have every acre of his heritage back, including his pride.

The musical sound of her voice drifted across the drive as he looked on. To his surprise, the calf she'd been coaxing ventured her way like an overgrown puppy starved for attention. Which she practically slathered on as she reached through the fence with both hands and rubbed the youngster around the ears and face, all the while cooing in baby talk.

"Oooo, you sweet baby calfie," she was saying as the calf pressed close.

Just that quickly, every other cow and calf was at the fence, pushing in for their share. Her delighted, "Hi, y'all," grated only slightly on J.D.'s nerves. He didn't know whether to swear or get a camera. His cattle weren't pets, weren't treated like pets, and on their best days never behaved in any way that could remotely be considered petlike. Yet, there they were, crowding around Zoe Yahzoo like a litter of pups for a scratch behind the ears or a silly word.

Her strange power over the stock made him uneasy. Particularly since his insides were humming in response to the sweet lilt of all that baby talk. Compelled to put a stop to it, he started the sorrel in her direction.

*　　*　　*

Zoe heard the sorrel's approach and glanced briefly over her shoulder. Realizing she might be overheard, she turned back to the cattle, bid them a whispered goodbye, then gave several hurried pats of farewell.

She wasn't as relieved as she should have been to finally have someone notice her arrival. Largely because she was certain the unfriendly looking cowboy on the sorrel was John Dalton Hayes. That J.D. Hayes was antagonistic toward a partnership with her had been made clear by her lawyer, so she guessed this first meeting with him would be difficult.

But then, she acknowledged with a wry inward smile, she'd faced difficult situations more times in her twenty-three years than most people imagined. Perhaps she'd reach her quota this time and be spared the most potentially devastating opportunity just ahead, the one she was forced to confront before she was ready.

And all because Zoe Yahzoo's time was running out.

She took a scant moment to start a smile, then turned toward the big man astride the sorrel who'd stopped just behind her. She came eye-level with a muscular thigh encased in batwing chaps. Her shaded eyes slipped to the cut-out front of the chaps, which were the unintentional frame of the man's masculinity, then up his green plaid shirt, which had no doubt been custom-made to accommodate such wide shoulders. She had to tip her face up so far to see his expression that it made her dizzy.

Dark sunglasses met dark sunglasses. Zoe flashed him an engaging smile, then turned up the dazzle when his jaw hardened and he glared forbiddingly down at her.

For a fractured moment out of time, she was cast back to her childhood. She must have looked up just as far at her adoptive father when she was small; she was certain she'd got this same response, tried the same hopeful dazzle in her smile to garner the tiniest bit of softening, and met with the same devastating failure.

But she'd learned something from all those heartbreaks, learned to give the appearance that she was either impervious to rejection, or oblivious. She'd watched her adoptive parents, probably the most talented actors of stage and screen, and had picked up enough acting ability to project any illusion she chose. And the illusion she'd chosen to project was the playfully flamboyant, tin-foil shallow, Zoe Yahzoo.

"Can I help you with something, miss?" The gravelly drawl was distinctly unfriendly.

Zoe turned up the wattage on her smile when his expression remained formidable and he refused to show her the courtesy of dismounting for a proper introduction.

"I was waiting for someone to come along. There didn't seem to be anyone home when I knocked." She put up her hand to offer him a handshake. "I'm Zoe Yahzoo. I think you must be J.D. Hayes." Zoe felt the rebuff when J.D. made no move to shake her hand.

"Sorry," he said, instead touching a finger to his hat brim in a way that communicated how thin the polite gesture was meant to be. "I've been working. My hands are dirty."

Zoe withdrew her hand, careful not to give any hint she'd noticed the insult. "Well, as far as that goes, I'm not sure how clean my hands are." She gave him an impish grin. "Your cattle are a bit dusty, Mr. Hayes. Perhaps we should postpone the proprieties until we've both had time to freshen up."

J.D. glanced away. It was a signal of irritation. Zoe automatically followed the shift of his attention and spied three ranch hands nearby who had evidently come out of hiding.

"If you could spare someone to help me with my luggage, I'll get settled in," she offered.

J.D. shook his head and raised his voice enough to be heard by his ranch hands. "I can't spare anyone to help you right now." J.D.'s words caused every man there to suddenly vanish, as if they were duty-bound to make true every word that came from his lips.

The absolute rule J.D. would have to have, to accomplish what she'd just witnessed, was impressive. It was also hurtful. But then, she'd expected to take some painful hits. And J.D.'s efforts were nothing compared to what she expected to receive from the people she'd come here to meet if they refused to accept her. This hostile partnership with J.D. was merely a means to an end, something she would endure to achieve her real purpose.

His full attention returned to her and his mouth quirked in faint mockery. "We don't have bellhops on Hayes, Miss...Yahzoo. My housekeeper keeps my house and cooks meals I like at times I set. She doesn't carry luggage, won't wait on you hand and foot, and God help you if you mess up her kitchen, sleep till noon or bitch about her cooking."

J.D. was as subtle as a freight train. Zoe gave him a cheeky smile. "I appreciate knowing where I stand, Mr. Hayes. Where do you suppose your housekeeper would like me to put my things?"

J.D. didn't hesitate. "In California."

Zoe made herself give a light laugh. "You have a sense of humor, Mr. Hayes. I appreciate that in a man." She punctuated the words with a flirtatious pat on the knee of his chaps and stepped around the sorrel.

The air fairly cracked with surprise as she strode to her car for the first of her things. She hefted out two suitcases and lugged them to the huge porch that wrapped around the Victorian ranch house before she turned back toward the car and dared a peek to see where J.D. had gone.

J.D. hadn't gone anywhere. He'd pivoted his sorrel and watched from where she'd left him at the fence, stunned at the idea that she'd not turned a hair at his rudeness, then gave him a brazen smack on the knee before she'd waltzed off. Volcanic wasn't a strong enough description for the sensation that had stormed through his system and short-circuited his nerve endings.

It must also have short-circuited his brain, he realized grimly, because his conscience was making a ruckus. He'd been too rough on her. Letting her move that small mountain of luggage into the house by herself might be overdoing it. Particularly if she dragged it in and unloaded it in the wrong bedroom. He was the one with the beef against her. It wouldn't be fair to set her up on Carmelita's bad side. Besides, Ms. Hollywood was probably spoiled enough to accomplish that on her own.

J.D. urged his sorrel across the drive to the grass and dismounted, leaving the reins dragging. Zoe was hefting another bag from the back seat and he took it from her smoothly with a gruff, "You get the small stuff." She said nothing, but rewarded him with a toothpaste-commercial smile.

Zoe sensed the difference in J.D. At best, it was only a minimal softening, but it soothed the sting of his antagonism. The small mountain was moved efficiently to the porch, then carried inside.

Zoe removed her sunglasses and took a brief glance around while J.D. went back after the last box. The two-story house was decorated with a hodgepodge of heavy masculine furniture that must have spanned every generation of Hayes ownership. Only a few pieces showed feminine influence, but each one, from the curved glass china closet she spied through the wide dining room door, to the delicate rocking chair in front of the hearth, took obvious pride of place.

Zoe wondered if the Hayes women had influenced their husbands and occupied their lives in those same proportions. If so, it wasn't surprising that J.D.'s ex-wife bore him such enmity. Zoe knew what it was like to be relegated to a trivial corner of someone's life; she was intimately acquainted with the pain and resentment that caused.

Her speculations vanished the moment J.D. entered the house and, because his path to the stairs was blocked by her things, sat the box down near the door. She watched with interest as he pulled off his sunglasses and stashed them in a shirt pocket. There was nothing now to conceal or soften his hard expression.

Eyes as dark and brown as she'd ever seen took her measure from the crown of her head to her boots. Wide, well-defined brows formed a nearly straight slash across his strong forehead. His face was ruggedly male, tough, his cheekbones high. Unsmiling, there was clear evidence of deep, cheek-climbing creases beside his firm mouth. It struck Zoe that J.D. was a younger version of actor Tommy Lee Jones. She was instantly attracted.

J.D. wasn't happy. He didn't want to analyze the depth of that unhappiness, but as he stared over in secret dismay at his new partner, he sure as hell knew its source. From her perky wedge of platinum curls to her neon blue eyes and delicate features, Zoe Yahzoo was more perfect and more female than any woman he'd ever laid eyes on. And as his vision was again seduced downward to the petite body below her remarkable face, his libido took extreme note of each delectable curve, all the way down the length of her thighs, knees and ankles until it reached the toes of boots so small she must have got them off a children's rack.

The flowery musk of light perfume that had already driven him nuts wafted his way on a fresh cloud and made his mouth water. Suddenly famished, the small plump curves of her breasts drew his gaze upward, but it was the happy dance of all those platinum curls when she tugged off her Stetson and tossed it to a table that helped him tear his attention from places it shouldn't have wandered in the first place.

The compulsion to put more than his attention on all those places was unlike any male urge he'd had in all his thirty-four years. A thundering heartbeat later, he realized that any trouble a woman had ever given him—including Raylene—was minimal compared to the potential for trouble this one presented.

J.D. breathed a silent curse and consigned his lusty thoughts to hell. He would never again allow his libido to overrule his good sense. The next woman he let himself be attracted to had to have dark hair, a mousy disposition, and no ambitions beyond a half dozen babies and entering pies at the county fair.

Zoe felt chastened by J.D.'s severe expression. She'd been scorched by the bold stroke of that blatant male gaze and felt a decided weakness in her knees. Her breath caught when he suddenly started her way, easily negotiating the obstacle course of her belongings with those long powerful legs. She couldn't get a full breath until his harsh gaze released hers to focus on the luggage nearest the steps.

Still a bit giddy from being on the receiving end of
J.D.'s sensual scrutiny, Zoe picked up two small cases
and trailed after him as he led the way up the stairs.
He'd managed to somehow take most of her luggage at
once by stuffing a piece under each arm and carrying
the handles to three suitcases in each of his big hands.
Zoe had never been particularly attracted to large muscular men, but the difference in J.D.—that he'd come
by his physique via a combination of genetics and hard
work—impressed her enormously. A man like J.D.
wouldn't need to pump iron under the watchful eye of
a trainer.

Oh, no, she thought with a burst of merriment. J.D.
had likely gotten his by bull-dogging steers all day and
wrestling bulls on weekends.

Zoe didn't realize she was grinning until J.D. stopped
and turned to glance back at her as he stepped sideways
through a door with his load. Zoe quailed inwardly at
the mighty frown he sent her. She made a valiant effort
to sober her expression, but nervousness defeated her.
Luckily, J.D. was through the door and was no longer
looking.

Zoe followed him into the room, then almost collided
with his big body. She lurched to a halt, her nose a scant
two inches from his wide chest. Her first impression was
that the green plaid wall in front of her smelled of sweat,
leather and sunshine, and that it was as solid as oak.
That it also radiated heat like a furnace didn't escape
her notice. Her hopes that the heat wasn't a barometer
of his temper died quickly.

"Miss Yahzoo." J.D. hesitated enough before he
growled "Yahzoo" to give the definite signal that he
found the name irksome. "In Texas, most *ladies* avoid

following strange men around with that kind of look on their faces.''

Zoe quickly set her suitcases down and traced the row of green buttons to his face. Brutal was somehow the only way she could describe his frown this time. She hoped she could make her expression serious enough to appease him.

''My apologies, Mr. Hayes. I meant no offense.'' The moment the words were out of her mouth, an explosion of nervous hilarity burst up. The best she could do to stop it was to bite the insides of both cheeks and make as dignified an escape as she could. Thank heavens there was still some luggage to bring up.

Zoe's amusement wound down by the time the last of her things was carried upstairs. In spite of those moments when J.D. had cast a lustful look at her, he was clearly not favorably impressed with anything else about her. Evidence of that was the way he'd simply exited the room once he'd unloaded the last box. He'd not spared her another word, much less a glance, and Zoe was stunned at how much his dislike unsettled her.

Zoe unpacked in record time, considering the number of things she'd brought with her. The room and its private bath were done in yellow rosebud wallpaper, the heavy woodwork painted a glossy white to match the high-gloss white paint on the restored triple dresser, night tables and armoire. The bed was a queen-size brass bed with elaborately curved metalwork and was, along with the rosebud lamps, the only new piece in the room. White pricilla curtains at the windows completed the cheery effect. It was all a nice contrast to what she'd seen so far.

She hurried downstairs, then discovered J.D. had left the house. A quick glance outside told her the sorrel was gone. A bit disappointed that he had abandoned her after their less than cordial beginning, Zoe went back upstairs to change into work clothes.

When she stepped out of her room later and started downstairs, she sensed by the silence of the big house that she was still alone. For all she knew, J.D. wouldn't be back anytime soon. She guessed he wouldn't appreciate her initiating her own tour of the ranch, but at least she was dressed for it.

She'd expected resistance when she'd bought into the ranch. Her lawyer hadn't needed to fill her in on any of that since she'd heard the circumstances from the California Realtor she'd hired to find her a rural house to rent here in Texas. She'd hoped to find something close by. When she'd discovered she could actually buy into the very ranch her young brother and sister lived on, she'd initially rejected the notion. But once the Realtor had told her that a group of environmentalists had raised funds to buy into Hayes, she'd reconsidered. Because of her, the people on Hayes were going to be drawn into enough trouble and scandal. Since she'd had the financial means to spare them further upset, she'd used it.

Zoe gave a grim sigh. She'd used her small fortune to manipulate people and circumstances, something she normally despised since it was a tactic her adoptive parents used as regularly as credit cards. That she'd done it for a good purpose made it only marginally better in her mind, though she imagined if J.D. knew what she'd done his reception to her that day would have been a good deal more congenial.

Zoe hadn't anticipated the impact he'd made on her. Aside from his close resemblance to one of her favorite actors, J.D. wasn't the socially polished, civilized type of man she'd been attracted to in the past. He was a huge man, wide-shouldered, narrow-hipped, with a hard strength that was evidence of his outdoor life-style. He was no gentleman rancher, content to sit on the porch while hirelings did the chores. He was too rough for that, too elemental.

And yet, in spite of his harsh manners, it was his inability to let her carry things into the house by herself that made a favorable impression on Zoe. However hostile he might be toward her, he'd not been able to bring himself to be a total cad. He'd been rude and aloof when she'd introduced herself, but she was suddenly glad he hadn't faked a welcome he didn't mean.

Something inside Zoe relaxed at that. All her life she'd had to be wary of anyone who paid her notice. Her adoptive parents were celebrities, and though she'd existed on the periphery of their charmed lives, the number of people who'd tried to get close to her to find favor with them had been legion. She sensed J.D. didn't give a rip about social climbing, wouldn't give a damn for hobnobbing with the rich and famous. His career was in land, cattle and oil, so there would be no value to linking his name with Jason and Angela Sedgewick.

On the other hand, he would be relating to Zoe Yahzoo as a person. Zoe saw no point in tipping the odds in her favor by revealing the fact that she'd been the better of his two buyers, not yet. If possible, she wanted a chance to be accepted for herself, though even she at times wasn't completely certain who that was. Zoe Yahzoo wasn't a total illusion, she knew that. She sensed her natural personality was lighthearted and sparkling, but pain and pride had intensified it so much that Zoe often felt like a fake.

Which was part of the reason she'd come here as she had, intending to get to know the people she was so obsessively curious about before her secrets were revealed to the world.

Of course, she acknowledged to herself, there was also the very real possibility they'd want nothing to do with her. Particularly considering the magnitude of the notoriety that would soon shadow her every move. Zoe tried not to give in to the anxiety that accompanied the reminder.

Zoe wandered through the living room, not comfortable familiarizing herself with the rest of the big house without a guide. She did find the kitchen, however. It was a large room, remodeled from what it once must have been, boasting custom-made wood cabinets and enough counter space to land a small plane. It was also immaculately kept, without a shred of clutter beyond a colorful assortment of cookbooks that crowded two long shelves. Zoe set her Stetson on a counter and got out a glass for water.

As she turned on the tap, she considered again the wisdom of keeping her identity a secret for a few more days. Memories of the show of affection her parents made when cameras rolled or others looked on gripped her for several moments. Sadness permeated the images, reaffirming her decision. Whatever the response of her birth family, acceptance or rejection, she had to know. She could no longer bear for anyone to feign affection for her because it made them look good or because it might gain them an advantage. It would be just as bad if they felt they had to manufacture feelings because of blood ties.

Resolved, she turned off the tap and had a long drink of water, grimacing a bit at the different taste. The door to the back porch opened, and she started guiltily. The impression J.D. had given her of his housekeeper made her leery of getting on the woman's bad side, but she collected herself and turned. Surely the woman wouldn't begrudge her a glass of water.

Only it wasn't the housekeeper who stepped inside. J.D. stood just inside the door, his six-foot-plus height dominating the kitchen she'd thought so large just moments ago. The welcoming smile Zoe sent him nearly faltered.

His dark eyes pinned hers. "You gonna leave that convertible out there like that?" His question came out more belligerently than he'd intended, but there was no sign in those remarkable blue eyes that he'd either riled her or hurt her feelings.

Zoe shrugged. "Is it in the way?"

J.D. reached up and yanked off his hat, then tossed it toward a counter. The slant that came to his mouth hinted at amusement. "Not unless you count birds and pigeons." He crossed the kitchen and Zoe stepped aside as he got out a glass. He moved to the refrigerator, opened the freezer door to scoop out some ice cubes, then stepped to the sink to fill the glass.

That she didn't fall all over herself to rescue her car from bird droppings intrigued J.D. He turned to lean against the counter and sample the water while he waited for a reaction. When she remained less than two feet away, leaning against the counter that was at right angles to the one he was backed up to, he decided Hollywood socialites didn't know too much about the big outdoors. And that meant any nasty little surprises that dropped on or in that red speed buggy would diminish her notions about ranch life. That, he was all for.

Zoe took note of J.D.'s speculation and the dark glint in his eyes that passed for humor. Though she guessed his amusement was at her expense, it was evidence of a sense of humor, however bent. Her nerve endings were sizzling from standing in his close proximity. And when those dark eyes made another bold head-to-toe sweep, she was reminded he wasn't entirely antagonistic toward her.

What she needed to know was how much of that antagonism he'd passed to others on Hayes. If J.D. had cast her too deeply in the role of wicked witch, it might prove difficult, if not impossible, to win over the very people she'd come here to find. She smiled at him to cover her anxiety.

"What have you told your people about me, Mr. Hayes?"

Her question hardened his expression. "No more than I had to," was his rough reply.

"Can you tell me...specifically?"

There was little more than a flicker of vulnerability in that tiny pause, but something in J.D. was alert to it. Every question he'd had about the reasons a Hollywood socialite would buy into a Texas ranch, then show up to live there, flashed through his mind, stirring his suspicions afresh. All at once he saw that her toothpaste-commercial smile was fake. Just as swiftly, he got a clear sense of the vulnerability it covered.

"Look, Ms—" J.D. hesitated irritably, as if he couldn't quite bring himself to say "Yahzoo." "Raylene made sure folks knew she turned my pockets out and got a third of Hayes in the divorce. The local paper printed the story of her selling it to someone from Hollywood. My foreman knows you were arriving today, my men have been wondering what the hell a Zoe Yahzoo is, and my housekeeper threatened to quit if you claim to have been abducted by aliens.''

Zoe giggled at J.D.'s grumpy humor. All was well. Pride had kept him from making too many negative remarks about his new partner. If the circumstances about what he'd lost in his divorce were that well known, the only face-saving thing left for him to do was to keep his objections—and disparaging comments about her—to himself.

"And what about you, Mr. Hayes? What were you expecting?"

He pressed his lips together in a disgruntled line and didn't answer.

Zoe studied him before she said quietly, "I'd like to hear it."

Silence dominated those next moments. Zoe waited, willing herself not to fidget. J.D. looked as if he wanted to let her have it with both barrels, and it might take everything she had to maintain her smiling facade. "Mr. Hayes?"

J.D. set his water glass on the counter, then brought his gaze back to hers. His look was level and hard, but his gravel-edged voice was surprisingly soft. "I was expecting a pain in the ass."

His statement, blunt as it was, didn't hurt her feelings. Mainly because she sensed it was not meant to. It occurred to her that he saw himself as the main target for his anger, since his own actions were responsible for the situation he was now faced with. There was something fair-minded about that and Zoe's attraction to him deepened.

"I'll try not to be a pain, Mr. Hayes," she said, though she knew because of the revelations that were coming, it was inevitable.

"Then sell out to me." There was steel in his tone and the look in his dark eyes was utterly determined.

Zoe was flustered into the slip, "Not yet," then recovered herself and started to step away from the counter.

J.D. noticed and seized her wrist to halt her retreat. "Not yet? Explain that."

Zoe turned fully toward him, unable to evade that penetrating glare. And the feel of those hard fingers wrapped so firmly around her wrist was nothing if not electrifying. Somehow, she regained her composure.

"I mean, when I'm ready to move on, I'll sell only to you, fair market value."

The light in his eyes blazed higher. "Why not now?"

"I want to be here now."

A frown line divided the space between his dark brows. "I want my ranch back. All of it."

"Enough to let me stay on peacefully?"

"Why the hell should I?" he demanded, clearly tantalized by the hint she didn't plan to stay forever, but frustrated because he had an indefinite wait to endure.

"Because I'm asking, Mr. Hayes," she said softly.

His voice went low, to an almost intimate growl. "And why should I do you any favors?"

Sensuality was so thick between them suddenly that the air was hard to breathe. J.D.'s fingers had somehow become a warm caress on the tender flesh of her inner wrist.

Her voice was barely above a whisper as she acknowledged, "I guess from your point of view, there's no reason."

J.D. gave her a sarcastic, "You're my partner."

"Not your adversary," she countered. "I don't want to take over, I don't want anything more than for you to honor the fact that we have a legal paper that gives me the right to live here. I'd like for you to allow me to do that in peace. You'd still be the boss."

J.D. gave a snort. "You're damned straight."

Zoe's smile was genuine and delighted, breaking the tension of those last moments. She gave him a sideways look. "Are you a tyrant, Mr. Hayes?"

Surprise flickered across his hard features, but he responded instantly with, "I'm a despot, Miss...Yahzoo."

"Can we get along peacefully?" she pressed.

"That remains to be seen."

Zoe considered a moment. "Fair enough."

He released her wrist slowly. There was no mistaking the heat that lingered in J.D.'s eyes, or the shivery tingle that zoomed through her in response. Zoe turned away and reached for her hat in a way that she hoped was a frivolous dismissal of the sensual undercurrent between them.

"Do you have time to show me around?" She settled her hat on her head and glanced back at him.

Unable to keep from tracking her every move, J.D. yanked his gaze from his avid contemplation of her backside to meet hers. His defensive, "Looks like you're dressed for it," amused her and she gave him a smile that let him know it before she let herself out the back door.

J.D. expelled a harsh breath that ended in a snort of self-directed disgust. As lustful as his relationship with Raylene had been in the beginning, it was little more than mild indigestion compared with the conflagration that had roared to life the moment he'd touched Zoe Yahzoo.

And if his instincts were right, he'd just got his first taste of the hell he'd have to suffer to honor her request to stay on peacefully.

CHAPTER TWO

J.D. FOLLOWED her out of the house, taking what he hoped was clinical note of her changed attire. Gone was the western chic outfit she'd arrived in. That black Stetson she had on now showed the unmistakable marks of long use, as did the brown work shirt, well-washed Levi's and the pair of scuffed brown boots. Even with her short wedge of curls and peaches-and-cream complexion, she looked as at home in work clothes as she had in her dude outfit. He resisted the urge to ask where she'd got the secondhand duds. Instead, he fell into step beside her on their way to the barns, resolving to keep her as far out of his line of sight as possible.

Zoe listened as J.D. gave her a brief overview of acreage, head of cattle and number of active oil wells and output. She looked on with interest as he walked her through the barns, stables and outbuildings. Every structure was in good repair, every horse still at the stables or in corrals in top condition. What cattle she could see, she recognized as Santa Gertrudis, and listened with only half an ear to the breed's advantages. Though J.D. wasn't boastful, there was an undercurrent of pride in his voice she suspected he was completely unaware of. She, on the other hand, loved his low-pitched drawl, content to stroll at his side and let the lazy sound of it flow over her.

She glanced his way, then had to look up quite a distance to see his profile. Her attraction to J.D. was a pleasant distraction. Never in her most grandiose dreams about finding her family had she imagined anyone else would so capture her attention. All her life she'd lived among some of the most charismatic people in the world, beautiful people who were so glamorous they weren't quite real.

J.D. was as rugged as a granite avalanche. There was none of the beefcake handsomeness of a Hollywood leading man, but J.D. was one of the most visually compelling men she'd ever met. His stern personality only enhanced his appeal. After dealing with shallow personalities and celebrity facades, people like John Dalton were nearly as overwhelming as they were a relief, and Zoe cautiously appraised him.

Money, fame and celebrity wouldn't impress him. Those were transient things, more fluke of nature than the norm. To a man with both boots set squarely in the stark reality of ranch living, hard work and good character would be the yardsticks he measured others by.

Zoe felt adrift suddenly, uncertain there was anything about her that a man like J.D. would respect or value. And if she couldn't earn his respect and regard, would she be able to earn those things with her birth family?

A lifetime of insecurity burst up and settled like lead in her chest. Money, fame and celebrity—but more particularly, the Sedgewick name—had gained her whatever acceptance she'd enjoyed. The Sedgewicks themselves had denied her admission to their hearts, but the rarified life they'd bestowed on her had guaranteed her entry nearly everywhere else. Zoe was abysmally aware that on her own, without the Sedgewick name and fortune, she might never have attracted the notice of most of the people she'd ever known.

Even her name change when she was eighteen and determined to get back at her parents had only hyped her celebrity with everyone else. Whatever fascination she'd attracted as the only daughter of the Sedgewicks soared to near star status once she renamed herself. Every talk show that had ever done a program on the children of celebrities pestered her, gossip columnists tracked her every move, and Zoe Yahzoo was on the A-list of every celebrity bash in the country. She charmed, she entertained, a pseudo-star at the edge of her parents' universe.

But none of that would mean anything on the Hayes Ranch. Not yet. She was merely the new co-owner, a rich Hollywood oddball with a crackpot name. And when Zoe Yahzoo's secrets were revealed to the world, the Hayes Ranch would share ground-zero status with the scandal that would rock Hollywood. Zoe felt a fresh sting of despair and forced those dismal thoughts to stop.

J.D. was saying something and it was suddenly vital to listen to his every word. She looked his way, then was snared by what she read in his dark eyes. Solid, stable, hard to win. Character traits Zoe found absolutely irresistible. The sudden knowledge that J.D. was somehow both a signpost and a turning point in her life stunned her. That she hadn't the vaguest clue as to what to do with the knowledge was terrifying.

"We need to get you started on riding lessons right away," he was saying, his statement startling her, particularly when he added the dig, "Unless you'd planned to lay around the house in the air-conditioning the whole time."

Zoe shook her head and proclaimed, "Oh, no, Mr. Hayes. I mean to live here and participate fully."

J.D. ignored the "participate fully" part. That was out of the question. It was reasonable though, for her

to learn to ride. Carmelita might not take to having Ms.
Hollywood underfoot the whole time.

"Then you'll need lessons," he insisted.

Zoe shook her head again. "I'm a fair rider, J.D."

He gave her a narrow glance and a skeptical twist of
lips. "A fair rider, huh?"

Zoe grinned up at him. "You can judge for yourself."
She headed for the stable, leaving J.D. to follow. When
they stepped inside and started down the aisle, Zoe asked,
"Can I choose my own mount?"

When she turned to him suddenly, J.D. abruptly
stopped. He gave her a stern look from his superior
height. "Depends on which one you choose," he said
gruffly. Zoe smiled at him, then paced down the aisle,
peering into the stalls on her way past, then turning to
come back to one of the first ones.

Inside, a muscular bay gelding with a wide blaze
looked out at her with interest. Zoe glanced J.D.'s way.
"How about this one for now?"

J.D. seemed to consider a moment, then gave a faint
nod. "Go ahead and choose your tack. You'll have to
saddle him yourself, then make sure he's properly put
up later. My men are cowboys, not maids." He leveled
her a meaningful look. "Or nannies."

Zoe ignored the gibe and was off toward the tack room
returning moments later with a saddle and bridle. J.D.
had taken himself off somewhere, so Zoe unlatched the
stall gate and stepped inside. She took a few moments
to get acquainted with the bay, then slipped the bridle
on smoothly and led him from the stall.

After a quick grooming, she reached for the saddle
blanket and closely inspected it before she tossed it
on the horse's back. J.D. had returned by then, leading
his sorrel.

J.D. watched critically as Zoe hefted the saddle atop the bay, impressed in spite of himself at her quick, competent work. He could find no fault with her skill so far, which added favorably to his private observation that she'd made a good choice with the bay.

Brute was a spirited horse, young, but with enough cow savvy and heart to satisfy J.D. That he often used the horse himself was testament to his regard for the animal. It was interesting that Zoe had chosen him, particularly when he suspected she was a weekend rider at best.

Zoe finished with the saddle. J.D. looked on as she took a moment to adjust the length of the stirrups, then turned toward him. "All set."

Her thousand-watt smile was back, he thought sourly, then was struck by the idea that there was something about Zoe that was familiar to him. The impression became stronger as they left the stable, leading their horses down an alley that bisected the network of corrals. He glanced her way more than once, looking for something specific to recognize, some special image that would confirm the notion. Though he was no avid fan of movies or TV, he'd watched his share during slow times of the year. She was starlet material in his book with those platinum curls and that movie star face. Looking at her didn't spark any particular memory, but the sense that he remembered her from somewhere was growing stronger by the moment.

They didn't mount until they were through the last gate and the vast expanse of range that surrounded the ranch headquarters stretched before them. J.D. turned to his horse. He'd no more than got his foot in the stirrup when Zoe was in her saddle, leaning forward to whisper something that sounded like nonsense in Brute's ear.

She gave the bay a pat, then straightened and glanced his way. "Ready?"

He couldn't have missed the eagerness on her face. J.D. nodded grimly and they set off at a slow pace.

Uncertain of her ability on the lively bay, he monitored her closely. He was determined for her to tire of ranch life and sell out to him at the earliest possible moment, but he didn't want her to get hurt.

And because he had no desire to see her hurt, it didn't bother his conscience in the slightest to use this opportunity to chafe a bit of the rosy glow off Ms. Hollywood's romantic notions about playing cowgirl. If she was the once-around-the-park weekend rider he figured she was, keeping her in the saddle for the entire four hours between now and supper might serve his purpose nicely.

Feeling charitable suddenly, J.D. glanced Zoe's way and gave her a rare smile. Zoe's thousand-watt response was blinding, giving him fresh hope that this perky little daffodil would wilt quickly and spare them both a long, hot afternoon in the Texas sun.

Zoe Yahzoo was a hell of a rider, J.D. concluded unhappily much later. He was hot and tired, bathed in sweat and gritty with dust as they headed to the cook house for supper. Zoe, he noted irritably, didn't sweat. Hell, no, he groused to himself, she got *dewy*. And the Texas dust that dared to land on that dew-kissed complexion managed to do so in such a way that could only be described as cute, with a streak here, a smudge there. It had surprised the hell out of him when she'd pulled out a hankie at the last stock tank and hadn't been squeamish at all about "freshening up" using the same water his cattle and horses drank from every day. It didn't fit his notion of how pernickety socialites behaved, even when they were playing cowgirl.

Worse, instead of being tired and whiny and sore from a hot afternoon on horseback, Zoe fairly bounced at his side, chattering in glowing terms about Brute and the ranch, as loose-limbed and invigorated as if it were a crisp fall morning following a long vacation.

He looked away from her high-energy exuberance, determined to keep from getting discouraged. She'd get tired of riding his horses. She'd be bored with Hayes in a week and get homesick for clean, lazy indoor afternoons in air-conditioning with house servants to cater to her life of ease. The social whirl of Hollywood would draw her back. Particularly since there was nothing on Hayes or in the vicinity that remotely resembled a celebrity party circuit.

J.D. comforted himself with that thought and the reminder that it was Carmelita's day off. They'd have to eat supper at the cook house. While Zoe had taken to him well enough, he was her co-owner, the boss, more in keeping with her station. She'd probably consider his ranch hands commoners. It would be interesting to see how this California glamor girl fancied sitting down to a table with that bunch, exposed to their rough manners while she faced a meal of red meat and potatoes.

They washed up at an outdoor spigot before they reached the cook house. J.D. got a step ahead of her as they walked up on the porch. He pulled open the screen door for her, then pushed open the inner door. Zoe flashed him a quick smile, then preceded him into the large dining room.

Ten of the ranch hands who lived on Hayes were already sitting around the long plank table. At the sight of Zoe, they jumped up almost in unison, causing an awful squall of the heavy backless bench seats as they were shoved back.

J.D. pulled off his Stetson and hung it on a nearby peg before he introduced Zoe. "Boys, I'd like you to meet Zoe Yahzoo. Miss Zoe will be sitting down to supper with us." He flicked Zoe a glance to see how she was taking his men, but Zoe had disposed of her Stetson and was stepping forward to shake the nearest man's hand.

She didn't give him a chance to introduce her to them separately, but asked for each name herself. She took her time working her way around the table, placing that small elegant hand in each blunt-nailed callused one as if she couldn't wait to make their acquaintance. That she was in no hurry was evident when she asked each man what they did on Hayes or if they had family nearby.

J.D. followed along until he reached the head of the table, where he waited to sit down until Zoe finished. Zoe appeared oblivious to the fact that the cook was about to sit the meat platters on the table, until she happened to see him, and turned to treat him to a smile.

"You must be the cook," she said brightly, then waited until Coley set the platters down before offering her hand and getting his name. "You set quite a table, Mr. Coley," she commented as she glanced over the table crowded with meat, potatoes, gravy, biscuits, four kinds of green vegetables and big bowls of canned peaches. "Is that apple pie I smell?"

The normally cantankerous Coley blushed, then blustered, "Ain't no Mr. Coley to you, Miss Zoe. Just Coley. And that's Dutch apple. I gotta couple gallons of home-made vanilla ice cream for the top, if'n ya ain't feared of spoilin' yer figure."

Zoe laughed. "If I put both gallons on my piece of pie, I probably would." She gave him a curious look. "Do you keep a lot of homemade vanilla ice cream around?"

"Sure do," Coley said, his chest puffed out a bit. "Make some nearly every day."

"Uh-oh, that was the wrong answer," she said with a groan and rueful shake of her head that indicated a weakness for homemade ice cream.

J.D. laughed along with the others, then waited until she made her way to the spot to his right that the men had left open for her on the bench. He was surprised at her reaction to his men, and couldn't help warming to her a bit despite the idea that meeting the ranch hands and sharing a meal with them didn't appear to dim her enthusiasm.

Zoe Yahzoo, despite her Hollywood background and starlet looks, was no snob. That his men were instantly taken with her was hardly a surprise, not when she looked like she did and had seemed so interested in getting acquainted with each one.

He looked on in silence as she bantered cheerfully at the table while she helped herself to generous portions and passed bowls and platters his way. She managed to mention enough names in her exchanges with his men to convince him that she remembered them all.

The men grew silent to eat and Zoe did, too. J.D. expected her to pick at her meal, but she packed away an astonishing amount of food for a woman whose slim figure suggested a careful diet. And when Coley brought in the pies and ice cream, Zoe helped herself again, not slowing until she'd finished every bite. She pushed her dessert plate away with a sigh and dragged her cup of coffee closer.

By the time they left the dining room to head back to the ranch house, Zoe's energy seemed to have wound down to an air of quiet contentment. J.D.'s mood darkened. Zoe was a hit with his men and his attraction to her was growing.

It aggravated him to realize that he was suddenly not as hot as he had been for her to sell to him and clear out. She was a bright curiosity to him, something new and decidedly foreign in his environment, yet she managed to fit in. No, he realized, she didn't fit in. It was more like she made a place for herself. He didn't have time to ponder that impression, because he glanced her way and saw her brow furrow thoughtfully.

"Didn't you mention having a foreman?"

They'd reached the back porch and he automatically opened the door to let her go ahead of him before he answered. "My foreman lives in the house by the highway. His son and daughter live with him, so they take their meals at home. He'll be around in the morning, if you're up."

Zoe managed to mask the tingle of anxiety and anticipation that went through her at J.D.'s first official mention of his foreman and his children. She'd been in suspense all afternoon and during the meal at the cook house for someone to mention Jess Everdine's name or his son's or daughter's. Since no one had, she'd finally had to ask something outright. Now she could force herself to get by the wait of one more night.

She couldn't, however, let J.D. get by with that "if you're up" wisecrack.

"Mr. Hayes." She hung her Stetson next to his on the wall pegs inside the kitchen, then turned to him with a chiding smile. "You seem to have a few unflattering ideas about me." She held up a hand to start ticking them off.

"Unless I want to lay around the house in air-conditioning, your men aren't maids, bellhops or nannies, *if* I'm up in the morning..."

He gave her a look from his height that seemed to emphasize his big stature.

She pointed up at him. "Ah, yes—that reminds me. There it is again, that superior look, that 'I'm the biggest gorilla in the jungle' pose."

J.D. gave her a bland twist of lips. "I thought you Hollywood types called them 'rain forests.'"

Zoe cringed and pressed a slim finger to her lips. "Ooops—don't tell."

"And what's wrong with acting like you're the biggest gorilla if you are?" he went on, the arrogant smile on his lips deploying the engaging creases that slashed upward to his cheekbones.

Zoe was staggered by the appeal of that smile and those deep-cut creases. J.D., gruff arrogance and all, would be an easy man to fall in love with. She laughed and couldn't resist flirting a bit.

"You've certainly made your point, Mr. Kong," she said as she leaned his way and nudged him with her elbow before she turned and started across the kitchen.

J.D.'s blood pressure shot roof high at that playful nudge. The fact that she'd immediately flitted away caused an instant frustration that made his breath catch. The woman was like the hot end of a downed high-voltage line, dancing and snapping, capable of frying a man alive the moment he came into contact with her.

He couldn't tear his eyes away, so it was a fresh shock to his system when she stopped at the door to the hall and looked back at him.

"I'm going to have an early night. Do you mind?"

He shook his head. "Not at all."

She gave him a smile that was not dazzling or commercial fake. "And thanks for letting your men meet me and form their own opinions. You could have so easily made having a good time with them tonight impossible."

J.D. couldn't respond to that. The utter sincerity and vague trace of wistfulness in those incredible eyes caught him as much off guard as her playful nudge had. He suddenly had the sense that this wistful, somber side of Zoe was the real thing. It contrasted sharply with all her bright smiles and good cheer, emphasizing the idea that there was much about the Zoe Yahzoo he'd seen so far that was somehow fake.

Words like glamor, image and pretense came to him. Words that suddenly didn't fit this strong impression of vulnerability. Even her soft, "Good night, John Dalton," touched him in that same peculiar way. He managed his own good night to her before she turned and disappeared through the doorway.

That night, J.D. dragged back the bedspread and top sheet, then fell into his big bed, worn out. Zoe's arrival and an afternoon in the heat had left him bone-weary, but he was too restless to fall asleep instantly. Instead, he stretched out and stared up at the darkened ceiling.

For the first time in what felt like years, he actually looked forward to the next day. He was anticipating it. Keenly.

He frowned, regarding that emotion with suspicion. From the day Raylene had walked out on him, he'd driven himself mercilessly, taken no time off, allowed himself few diversions. He was aware that his grueling routine was the means to both work off his anger at himself and do penance for his mistakes with Raylene,

but he'd thrived on it. He'd found a measure of satisfaction in pushing his limits, denying his emotional needs
and testing his mental and physical stamina until he'd
proven himself equal to the task. He hadn't needed
wimpy emotions like eagerness and anticipation to be
the engine for the way he'd lived his life.

He sure as hell didn't need them now, he assured
himself. But a quick flash of sunshine curls and laughing
blue eyes burst on his thoughts and made a lie of his
secret declaration.

From his first glimpse of her, Zoe had captured his
attention and given his austere emotions a banquet of
strong sensation to feast upon. She had a way of ab-
sorbing his focus that wasn't limited to or dependent on
her looks, though they were a hell of a draw. Her bright
personality, bouncing energy and cheerful humor were
enormously entertaining, but his insight into a more
somber Zoe was a contrast that fascinated him. She was
a shining oasis in the dry sand of his existence, and J.D.
was suddenly profoundly aware that he'd been slowly
dying of thirst.

He cursed and flopped over to pummel his pillow. For
a man not given to whimsy, he was practically infested
with it tonight. He was no navel-gazer, so he couldn't
account for this impulse to take stock of himself and
the way he lived his life.

That could only mean the blame for his mental and
emotional turbulence rested squarely on Zoe Yahzoo.
He'd expected her unwelcome presence to throw things
out of whack until he could get her to sell out and leave.
He hadn't expected her to throw him out of whack.

And the fact that she was completely responsible for
this gut-jumping anticipation for morning when he would

surely see her again made him give his pillow another surly punch.

At last, he got settled and expelled a deep, tired breath. Tomorrow he'd set himself—and her—to rights. He was boss of Hayes and boss of himself. There would be no more emotional disruptions, no more letting himself be distracted from his determination to have her clear out of his life. He'd make himself scarce for most of the day. By the time Ms. Hollywood got out of bed, he'd have eaten breakfast and would be a good three miles away.

Comfortable with that, J.D. closed his eyes.

CHAPTER THREE

ZOE didn't meet J.D.'s housekeeper, Carmelita Delgado, until breakfast that next morning. Though Zoe hadn't heard the woman come home the night before from her day off, she was on duty in her immaculate kitchen that morning, shoving a coffee cake into the oven at 5:05 a.m.

Zoe halted in the doorway, not wanting to startle the woman. She called out a soft, "*Buenos días, Señora Delgado*," then smiled when the woman turned from the oven, her dark brows raised in faint surprise. "My apologies, *señora*. I didn't mean to startle you."

"Do you know what time it is?" The question was almost a demand.

Zoe's brow crinkled slightly. She scanned the kitchen for the clock and checked her watch to compare the time. "It's 5:05. Am I late?" Her smile faded slightly at the intent way Carmelita was regarding her. Anxiety made a sharp pass through her middle. "Am I too early?" Zoe cast a belated glance around. "I see Mr. Hayes isn't here yet."

"Are *you* this Zoe Ya-hoo?" the woman asked in richly accented English, her dark eyes showing the tiniest bit of welcome with the surprise.

Zoe sat her saddlebags next to the table, then crossed the kitchen to shake Carmelita's hand. "That's Yah-*zoo*, but please call me Zoe. It's nice to meet you, *señora*."

Carmelita absently gave her hand a shake, seemed to see something she was looking for in Zoe, then pumped her slim hand vigorously. "Are you a movie star?" There was genuine interest in the woman's voice.

Zoe shook her head. "Not unless you count a one line part in a teen horror film when I was nineteen, and a few public service commercials."

Zoe hoped that would be enough to satisfy Carmelita's curiosity. She didn't want to deal with questions that demanded answers which would bring up the Sedgewicks, not yet. She knew she would have to mention them sometime, and soon, so that the people on Hayes would have some preparation for what was coming. But selfishly, if only for a little while, she wanted people to meet her and have a chance to get to know Zoe Yahzoo without the magic of the Sedgewick name to win them over.

Her resolve wavered when Carmelita suddenly asked, "Is your family named Yahzoo, or is your name made up?"

Zoe smiled and tried to evade the question by saying, "It's made up," but Carmelita was surprisingly persistent.

"What name is your family name, *señorita*?"

Zoe's breath seemed to lodge in her throat a moment before she could say, "Sedgewick. My parents named me Spenser Trevyn." She hoped the sheer snobbery of her first and middle names would distract Carmelita from the name Sedgewick. It was a futile hope.

Carmelita threw up her hands and let out a whoop before she grabbed Zoe's hands again. "Jason and Angela Sedgewick—" Whatever she'd been about to say ebbed into swift Spanish that Zoe couldn't follow too closely with her limited command of the language. She didn't need a translation to know the woman was making glowing comments, and Zoe couldn't help the disappointment she felt.

Carmelita switched back to English and fixed her with a puzzled look. "But why would you not keep your family name?"

Zoe gave her a wry smile. "Because when I was eighteen and in a very silly, rebellious frame of mind, I changed it."

The housekeeper drew back and placed her hand on her chest in surprise. She shook her head and gave Zoe a disapproving look. "This is not good, this dishonor to your parents."

Zoe's smile drifted away and she said quietly, "Perhaps not, *señora*. As I said, I was in a very silly, rebellious frame of mind." Zoe tried to redeem the confession Carmelita so clearly objected to. "And I can assure you, they greatly appreciate that the name Yahzoo is in the credits of that teen horror film, instead of theirs."

Before either of them could say more, a big voice sounded from the doorway. "So how come you didn't change your name back when you got over your rebellion?"

Startled, Zoe turned to see J.D. enter the room, his dark eyes making a brisk pass over her before he crossed to the coffeemaker to help himself to coffee.

"Maybe I never got over it," she answered swiftly, then went to take the steaming cup he held out to her. "Besides, I think even you have to admit that the name Spenser Trevyn Sedgewick stinks of elitist snobbery, not to mention raising questions of gender." Zoe laughed at the look that suddenly blunted his expression.

"But what the hell kind of name is Zoe Yahzoo?" he demanded, his big voice a deep growl.

"It's a fun-sounding name, Mr. Hayes. It's a name that reminds me not to take myself too seriously, particularly since I used to have a lot of problems doing just that." She grinned at him as if she wasn't making the somber revelation she really was.

But J.D.'s stare was intense and she had the unsettling feeling that he could see straight through her. She turned instantly to Carmelita.

"I can cook, *señora*. Would you like help with breakfast?"

Her offer seemed to break the loaded silence. Carmelita smiled and waved her off. "The boss will probably have you working hard enough today. Best you rest where it's quiet and cool while you can." With that, she went on with her meal preparations.

Zoe looked over at J.D. as they sat down across the table from each other. She raised her light brows and leaned forward conspiratorially. "Oooo, that sounds ominous, J.D. Do you have visions of sending me back to the house saddle-sore and whining by noon?"

"I won't be sending you back from anywhere, because you won't be working," he groused, then shot Carmelita a surly look for saying so. Carmelita wagged a fork at him and turned away.

Zoe took confidence from Carmelita's insubordination. "But I want to work, J.D. That's what I meant when I said I wanted to participate fully."

"I know what you meant," he said darkly as he reached for the newspaper and unfolded it. "But ranch work is hard and dirty and dangerous."

Zoe made a face of mock horror. "Oh, John Dalton— you aren't one of those Neanderthals who thinks women are too weak for men's work, are you?"

"I sure as hell am. Damned proud of it," he said with exaggerated boredom as he opened the paper and began to scan an inside page.

Carmelita gave an unladylike snort that drew Zoe's attention, but the housekeeper appeared to be absorbed with turning two breakfast steaks in the skillet.

She looked back at J.D. "What do you suggest I do all day?"

"Ride Brute, use the pool, run up the phone bill, do your nails—whatever you like as long as you don't get in anyone's way." His instant answer belied his concentration on the newspaper.

Zoe stared over at J.D.'s aloof expression as he scanned the paper, not certain if she was offended or amused. She decided not to protest just yet. She sensed there was a way around his refusal to let her do ranch work. Besides, proving she was not only experienced with ranch work, but reasonably competent wasn't uppermost in her mind just now. Getting a first glimpse of Jess Everdine and his children was.

Her blithe, "Okay," as she reached for a section of newspaper drew a suspicious glance from J.D. that she pretended not to notice as she opened the section and began to scan the print.

Breakfast was served shortly, and Zoe dug in, intending to fortify herself for the day ahead. She intercepted several dark looks from J.D., and responded with an airy smile to a few of them. By the time they finished eating, his expression was as black as a storm cloud. Zoe drank the last of her coffee and raised her light brows as she looked over at him.

"Something bothering you, J.D.?"

His answer was instant. "You."

"Me?"

His low growl was apparently a confirmation. "What are you going to do all day?"

She couldn't resist. "Ride Brute, use the pool, run up the phone bill, do my nails—mainly, I'll try not to be a pain in your backside, John Dalton." She gave him a bright smile. "Go on about your business, and don't give me another thought."

She stood and glanced over at Carmelita, who was assembling ingredients for what looked to be chocolate cake. "Thank you for breakfast, *señora*. You're a wonderful cook."

Carmelita smiled her thanks and went back to work. J.D. was getting to his feet when he took note of Zoe reaching for the saddlebags she'd set aside earlier.

"What have you got in those?"

Zoe gave him a chastening frown for his grouchy tone, then lifted them to the table. She tugged a thong, then flipped one side open to show him. "A compass, a map of Hayes, a snakebite kit, sunblock, a collapsible drinking glass, gloves." She paused to open the other side. "A steel thermos, sandwich box, granola bars..." She looked up and smiled. "Everything but a horse and a saddle to tie them to. All right?"

By the look on his face, it wasn't, but he nodded. "Just stay close to the house. It's too damned much trouble to organize a search party. Stay away from the cattle. If you open a gate, close it. Don't get in anyone's way, and don't stay out too long."

Zoe rolled her eyes and swung the saddlebags onto her shoulder, leaving the thermos out. "I don't suppose you'd care to have me tag along with you this morning," she said hopefully.

"We're moving cattle to another pasture first thing," he muttered. "It's hot, rough work on that part of the range and no place for a greenhorn."

She gave him a teasing smile, then took her thermos to the sink to fill it with water. "Perhaps you ought to see for yourself how much a greenhorn I am. I could wander off someplace with my map and compass..." She let her voice trail off meaningfully.

"Not if I restrict you," he said darkly.

Zoe flashed him a look. "Good luck with that notion."

J.D. frowned at her, then the saddlebags, and expelled a harsh breath. "Come along, then. But if you get in the way, I'll send you back to the house."

"Fair enough." She turned on the tap and filled the thermos before she twisted the cap on and secured it in the saddlebag. She hurried over to grab her hat from the peg, then followed J.D. outside, rushing to get ahead of him to retrieve a couple things from her car's trunk on the way past.

J.D. didn't remark when she got out a set of blunt-roweled spurs and a pair of batwing chaps as he passed by, but the coil of rope she'd slung over her shoulder by the time she caught up and fell into step beside him got an immediate response.

"Where the hell did you get that rope?"

"I bought it." Zoe ignored the dark look he sent her.

"You can leave it in the barn," he declared.

Zoe didn't argue, and when they reached the barn where four of the ranch hands were saddling up, she had no problem keeping the rope out of J.D.'s sight. She swiftly groomed and saddled Brute, fastened the rope and saddlebags to the saddle, then buckled on her spurs and got on her chaps.

That J.D. was accustomed to having his every edict obeyed to the letter was evident when he didn't bother to check to see whether she'd left her rope behind or not. By the time they left the barn, Zoe had forgotten about the rope herself. J.D. had said she'd meet his foreman if she was up early enough. She assumed this was early enough, since it was just past six o'clock. Her nerves were taut with suspense, but the only men she saw were the ones she'd met at supper the night before. It was on the tip of her tongue to ask J.D. about the foreman, but she decided such a question might attract attention.

The six of them were well away from the ranch head-quarters before J.D. looked her way.

"I thought I told you about that rope," he groused.

Zoe looked over at him and shrugged. "I figured you didn't realize that I use it for more than a prop. You said we were going to move cattle."

"When I said 'we', I didn't include you. What the hell would you know about moving cattle?" he challenged, then smirked. "Hayes isn't some gigantic petting zoo, Hollywood. You leave that damned rope tied on your saddle, or I'll take it away."

Zoe's smile was forced as she felt the heat of embarrassment climb her cheeks. The four men riding with them had heard every word.

They reached the pasture J.D. designated some time later. It was on a hilly section of the ranch. Stands of mesquite that provided shade punctuated the hills, some of the scrubbier stands making Zoe glad she'd taken note of J.D.'s chaps and worn her own to protect her legs. The pasture was large, and because of the small valleys between hills, finding the cattle and moving them would be a greater challenge.

Zoe tugged her hat down more firmly, then glanced over at J.D. The four cowhands with them fanned out in what must have been a prearranged pattern.

"Which direction are we moving them?" she asked.

J.D. gestured to the south. "That way." He gave her a stern look. "Ride with me, but stay out of the way."

Zoe did as he ordered, and they rode down a wide path that paralleled the distant fence that marked the west boundary of the section. They found eight head of cattle just past the shallow crest of the first hill. The small bunch started to mill when they noticed the riders' approach. Zoe held Brute back a reasonable distance from J.D.'s sorrel, leaving him to start the cattle in the direction he wanted. For now, she'd do as he said and stay out of the way.

She'd moved cattle before, so she was aware of how easily a stray or two could double back. Zoe had spent every summer since her ninth birthday on one ranch or another in Colorado, Texas, Wyoming or Montana. It had irked her parents that she'd been so in love with cowboy life that she'd wanted to live on ranches all summer. But the fact that they could ship her off anyplace that vaguely resembled the summer camp their friends sent their children to had made them tolerate her choice.

Zoe'd had the benefits of an outdoor life that was worlds different from the high-society pretense that had crushed her; her parents could turn her and a bucket of money over to someone else to bother with for the summer. They'd neither noticed nor cared that each year she'd requested to go to a new list of ranches, each one more of a working ranch than the ones before.

She'd known since she was small that her biological mother had grown up on a ranch somewhere. She'd overheard enough of Angela's disparaging comments about "Spenser's hayseed origins" to find that out. Ultra-refined Angela had been appalled at her repeated requests to spend summers on a ranch, railing at her husband about the poor breeding of the child he'd insisted they adopt. In the end, she'd given in, mainly because Jason had been feeling a rare occasion of pity for Zoe's emotional neglect. He'd finally decreed it as a kind of bribe.

And so had begun in earnest Spenser Sedgewick's childish search for her mother. Summer after summer, she'd lived on one ranch after another, getting to know everyone on the ranch and as many people in the area as she could. She'd searched every face, a naive child certain she'd know her mother on sight. Year by year, she'd watched for the woman who might be her mother, trying to find her in the only way a lonely child could. Hoping, wishing...

"Dammit, Zoe! Get out of the way!" J.D.'s shout yanked her from her thoughts in time to see one of the range bulls bearing down on her and Brute. Brute lunged to the side and Zoe kept her seat, pivoting the bay and automatically riding after the bull. Instinct rushed to the fore, both Brute's and hers as they raced fearlessly after the animal and came alongside. Almost without conscious thought, Zoe's rope was in her hand and she whacked the young bull on the neck, startling him into a turn. In moments they were chasing him back to J.D.'s gather. Zoe pulled back on the reins to let the bull slow and rejoin the bunch.

A scant moment later two cows broke to the right and Zoe angled Brute up the side of a hill to cut them off and start them back in the right direction. She took a position to the right rear of the gather and slapped her rope on the leg of her chaps as both a reminder to the cattle that she was there, and to make a sound that would keep them moving straight ahead.

The only note she took of J.D. was where he was riding in relation to the small herd. He had breakaways of his own to chase back, so he'd have little time to chastise her. Over the next hill, Zoe saw three more cows off to her right, closer to the boundary fence. After taking a quick glance at the cattle ahead to be sure they were moving along peacefully, she started Brute in their direction. While she was still a distance away, the three cows bolted the wrong way.

Zoe touched a spur to Brute, delighting in his quick reaction and impressive burst of speed. They rode to block the cows, and Zoe got a taste of Brute's cow savvy and agility as she gave him his head to work the cows, lunging and feinting, until all three cows turned tail. With no more than a bawl of protest, they moved off to join the gather.

Zoe grinned to herself, pleased. The trick of moving cattle was to do it with a minimum of fuss to avoid overtiring her horse and running weight off the cattle. By the time the three cows reached the others, Zoe had again taken up her right rear position.

J.D. was too surprised to be angry about Zoe's rope. She rode Brute like a pro and handled his cows as if she knew what she was doing. She hadn't been trying to defy him about the rope, and it was certainly no prop. His curiosity about her rose several more notches as he both watched for cattle to add to the gather and kept track of Zoe as she did the same.

By the time they reached the south gate, they had accumulated thirty head of cattle. His ranch hands hadn't arrived yet, so as soon as their cattle were through the gate, J.D. closed it and they rode back to join the others.

They had a busy morning, searching every valley and mesquite stand until the number of cattle they moved matched the tally of cattle that were supposed to be in this pasture. When the gate was finally closed and they started back, J.D. spoke.

"So, how many head of cattle do you Hollywood socialites run on those big fancy lawns out in Beverly Hills nowadays?"

Zoe laughed at J.D.'s question, delighted that his attitude toward her had brightened considerably, and that the four men who'd heard his warning about the rope now rode close enough to hear this, too. She got the strong impression J.D. was trying to make up for what he'd said earlier. It was also a wonderful acknowledgment that he credited her with at least a bit of skill.

"Not many," she answered, realizing with some surprise that she wanted J.D. to know something about her life. At least the better parts. He'd find out about the not-so-nice parts soon enough. "This socialite spent all her summers on working ranches that let wannabe cowgirls pay big money for the privilege of working as a hired hand."

One of the men with them swore in surprise, then blushed a deep red. "Beg pardon, Miss Zoe. You did a fine job this morning."

Zoe gave him a happy smile. "Thanks for saying so, Gus. That's a nice compliment from someone who does the work all the time." She faced forward, feeling a rare surge of contentment. She'd earned a bit of something with J.D. and these men this morning and it felt good.

But that feeling lasted only long enough for the headquarters to come into view. The people she'd come here to see were there somewhere. The foreman who may or may not be her natural father was the last of J.D.'s employees remaining for her to meet. The sharp needle of anxiety she'd managed to set aside while they'd moved the cattle was suddenly driving through her like a spear.

Once everyone knew who she was and realized the magnitude of trouble she'd brought to Hayes, she'd be lucky if any of them would have a good word to say to or about Zoe Yahzoo.

J.D. was alert to the mood shift in Zoe. Those megawatt smiles were coming more frequently, and her lighthearted facade seemed a touch more forced once they arrived back at the barn. Because he was watching more closely, he took grim note of the tremor in her hands as she unsaddled Brute. Something wasn't right, but he was distracted from further speculation.

"Mr. Hayes?" A boy's voice called from the open doors at the far end of the stable.

The sound of that voice struck something in Zoe's chest with the force of a blow. A soul-deep certainty that she'd never felt the like of, had her turning in wonder. A boy of about ten started down the aisle that bisected the stable, eagerness hurrying his steps until he reached J.D. Zoe turned Brute into the stall, then stepped into the shadows with him to peer out the rails.

"Mr. Hayes? You said you'd think about letting me build a tree house over in that one tree behind the east pecan grove." He dug in his back pocket and pulled out a paper that he quickly unfolded and held out to J.D. "I drew up the plan like you wanted." J.D. took the paper and examined it closely while the boy looked up into his hard features with a mixture of eagerness and hope.

Zoe stared. The boy was sturdy, of average height and build for his age. His shirt and jeans were already dusty and smudged with dirt from a morning of doing what boys did on ranches. His Stetson was tipped back on his head, and a few lanky strands of dark blond hair angled from a side part to lay in charming disarray across his forehead.

She didn't need to hear J.D. say the boy's name; she needed nothing more than hearing his voice and looking upon that young, handsome face to know who he was. For the first time in her twenty-three years, she was setting eyes on her own flesh and blood.

Zoe swayed with the force of the revelation, sagging dizzily against the rails of the stall. The search of a lifetime was suddenly centered on the boy with J.D., the years of brutal disappointment soothed away by this first glance. The pain of never meeting her mother face-to-face, the knowledge that now she never would, finally didn't feel so terrible. Something that was both tender and fierce twisted her heart, assailing her so spontaneously that it stole her breath.

Somehow, she kept from crumpling to the straw-strewn floor as she fought to get a grip on the emotions that were choking her. Somehow, she collected herself, and through sheer force of will, she wrestled Zoe Yahzoo's sparkling facade back into place and stepped out of the stall.

And without a moment to spare as J.D. gestured in her direction, prompting the boy to notice her. The sudden shyness that made Bobby Everdine snap his mouth shut and blush was endearing.

SUSAN FOX   53

Zoe closed the stall gate and picked up her saddlebags before she walked over, struggling to behave with some semblance of normalcy. J.D.'s dark eyes would catch anything unusual, particularly since she noted his attention was suddenly sharp on her flushed face. It wasn't time for anyone to figure things out. Not before she met Jess Everdine and found some way to talk to him first.

"Hello, there. W-who might you be?" she asked with a smile, secretly dismayed at her slight stammer.

J.D. took over the introduction. "This is Bobby Everdine, my foreman's boy." He placed a big hand on Bobby's shoulder. "And this is Miss Zoe Yahzoo."

Zoe put out her hand, unaware of its tremor as she gave Bobby a handshake. The contact was brief and she managed to release his hand at the appropriate time.

"Pleased to meet you, ma'am," he said awkwardly, his blush climbing a bit higher.

Zoe's heart was given an added twist. "Did I hear you say you're building a tree house?"

"*Might* be," he corrected, then shyly looked up at J.D. "But I gotta get permission."

Zoe turned to J.D., instantly taking the boy's side. "Every boy ought to have a tree house, John Dalton."

J.D.'s expression gave no clue to his decision as he looked from her to the boy. "What's your daddy say about this?" he questioned sternly.

"He said it was up to you, sir, since you own the tree." As if he sensed permission was coming, the eagerness in his eyes made their blue color sparkle with excitement.

"Where're you gonna get the wood and nails?" he questioned next.

"From the scrap wood they're gonna throw away from that new bowling alley. And I've been saving my allowance for the nails."

J.D. shook his head to that and Zoe's temper flared in indignation until he said, "There's plenty of scrap wood left over from the new stud barn. It's in the loft, in the way, so you'll have to get it down." He passed the boy's drawing of the tree house back to him. "There're weeds around the machine shed that need clearing. If you'll clean them out and rake the ground, the wood's yours and you can use as many of my nails as you need. You can borrow a hammer and hand saws, as long as you take care of them and put them back where they belong."

Bobby let out a whoop, his bright face lit by a wide smile. "Thanks, Mr. Hayes." He latched onto J.D.'s big hand and gave it a shake. "I'll get those weeds outta there right now." As if he couldn't wait to get started, he let go of J.D.'s hand and whirled around to run down the stable aisle. He got only a few strides before he skidded to a halt and turned back to look at Zoe. "Nice to meet you, ma'am," he called back, then spun around and tore out of the barn.

Zoe watched him go, her eyes smarting with unshed tears. She blinked them back and looked at J.D. "You're a nice man, John Dalton Hayes." She gave him a soft smile, then reached over to briefly touch his arm in a way that hinted at friendly affection. "So how about taking me to lunch? I'm so hungry even Brute was starting to look good."

J.D. wasn't fooled by that smile. His blood pressure was soaring as a result of another of Zoe's hit-and-run touches, but he wasn't about to be distracted from what he'd just witnessed. For all her playfulness and starlet looks, there was something melancholy and tender-hearted about Zoe Yahzoo.

Unfortunately for him, sensing that there was more to Zoe than megawatt smiles and disarming charm only made her that much more appealing. And as a man whose life-style had been disparaged and scorned by one woman, the idea that another had some fondness for it was one hell of a temptation.

CHAPTER FOUR

"YOU can park your car in the garage," J.D. told her as he quickly finished with his sorrel and turned the horse into his stall. "There's a spot for it on the east end."

Zoe looked on, still recovering from her brief meeting with her young brother. Her anxiety about meeting her sister and the man who might be her natural father was soaring. It was all she could do to keep from fidgeting with nerves, but she gave J.D. a grin.

"Thanks. I appreciate that, J.D. But you were wrong about the birds."

He gave a gruff chuckle and closed the stall gate. "You must lead a charmed life, Hollywood."

Zoe abruptly broke contact with the unexpected glimmer of humor in his dark eyes, saddened by the remark. That Zoe Yahzoo lived a charmed life was a lie. The worst sort of pretense and an overabundance of money had created that image. The world would be finding out the particulars very soon. Zoe was not only terrified of having that glittering veil yanked away, she wasn't certain how she would fare without it.

"That bother you?" J.D.'s low voice startled her from her thoughts, and she lifted her head to meet his close study of her.

Some instinct about J.D. urged her to dare a bit of candor, but the habits of a lifetime—not to mention cowardice—made her give him a bright smile to cover her offhand hint. "Charmed lives aren't all they're cracked up to be, John Dalton." She started down the aisle toward the far door and he fell into step beside her. "And because they aren't, I'll move my car to the garage—*before* lunch."

Zoe had dug her car keys from her pocket by the time they stepped out into the sunshine. She automatically glanced toward where her car was parked under the tree and faltered.

A girl of about seventeen—the same age as her sister— was standing beside her red convertible, looking it over. Wearing a white T-shirt and jeans, her western hat hanging down her back by a thong, the girl had the almost exact shade of blond hair that was also Zoe's natural color before she'd lightened it.

The same overwhelming certainty she'd experienced with Bobby—that she was looking upon her own flesh and blood—assailed her, with the same poignant twist of her heart. Zoe's breath caught, struck by the revelation that her sister, Rebecca, bore a strong facial resemblance to the high school yearbook picture Zoe had of their dark-haired mother.

As if surviving her first contact with her family made it easier the second time, Zoe recovered, and moved with shaky confidence toward her car.

"How do you like it?" she called out as she and J.D. came closer.

The girl glanced up, her pretty face alight. "It's a really neat car. It's yours?"

Zoe nodded and stopped next to the girl as J.D. made the introductions. "Becky Everdine, this is Miss Zoe."

Zoe waved away the formality. "It's just Zoe, and I'm pleased to meet you, too," she repeated back, nearly unable to keep from staring at the girl's face too long. Instead, she gestured toward her car. "Mr. Hayes just invited me to move it into the garage. Would you like to drive it over?'' She held up the keys.

Becky shot J.D. a shy look before her gaze fastened on the keys with instant longing. She shook her head with regret. ''I probably shouldn't.''

''Don't you have a driver's license?''

Becky glanced at the car. ''Yeah, but I'd be afraid of scratching it or something.''

Zoe smiled. ''It's insured, the garage is close, and I'm not a fanatic about dings and scratches. It's just a car.''

Becky turned back with a wry grin. ''But *what* a car!''

They both laughed at that, and Zoe shoved the keys in her direction. ''Go ahead and put it away. Just leave the keys in the ignition so I know where they are.''

''Well...'' She looked at Zoe, grinned the same impish grin Zoe had seen in the mirror on her own face, then took the keys. ''Okay!''

Zoe managed to maintain her smile and watched, unable to keep from staring as if she were memorizing every move and expression her sister made. J.D. remained silent beside her as Becky hurried around the car then opened the door and got behind the wheel. She looked over the dashboard gages and switches, then took a moment to run her hand over the white leather seat before she slipped the key into the ignition.

The engine hummed to life and Becky put the car into gear. Hesitating only long enough to give Zoe a smile and a wave, she started the car cautiously forward.

Zoe was so engrossed, she didn't notice anyone approach.

''That girl's been moonin' over that red convertible since you drove by our house yesterday.''

The deep drawl startled Zoe, and she turned toward it. A big man who rivaled J.D. for height stood no more than three feet away. A black Stetson didn't quite cover his telltale dark blond hair. The tanned, sun-lined face that looked over at her was smiling and friendly, the blue eyes that regarded Zoe only shades darker than her own. She knew instantly this was Bobby and Becky's father, Jess. The reminder that there was a chance that he might also be her father exploded on her consciousness.

Suddenly it was all too much. Weeks of dread and hope, a lifetime of hurt and longing, the relentless emotions that had both led her here and driven her, were overpowering. Everything she'd missed, everything she'd needed, was suddenly here at this moment in her life. The horror of being rejected by this man, the terror that he might forbid her contact with the only two people she was certain were related to her, combined with the emotional turbulence of that morning.

Zoe tried to smile, but the best she could manage made her lips tremble. Her knees went weak, and a new terror—that she was about to faint—overrode everything else. J.D.'s steady drawl as he introduced her to Jess Everdine, penetrated her dizziness and snatched her back from the edge.

"Pleased to meet you, Miss Zoe," Jess said as he offered his hand.

Zoe took it, gathered strength from his warm grip, and mumbled what she hoped was an appropriate response. Anything more was beyond her. She searched Jess's gaze, desperate for some spark of recognition, yet just as desperate for him to see nothing. She, on the other hand, was looking for any sign in his sun-weathered face, any clue that would tell her if he was her father. Though it was near certain he was, there was always the chance she was the product of her mother's intimacy with someone other than her high school sweetheart.

It was then that Zoe realized she'd gone about everything in the worst possible way. As she let go of Jess's hand, she couldn't immediately look away from the handsome face that bore both the squint lines of happiness and the grim etchings of hard times. Her impression of the man—that he was honest and straightforward—made the way she'd manipulated her way into his life suddenly seem a monstrous deception. The self-delusion that had fogged her judgment and urged her on began to evaporate and Zoe felt the shock to her toes.

She'd come here under false pretenses as J.D.'s new partner, determined to fully indulge her own selfish need for acceptance from her birth family before she let any of them know who she was. It was only now, at this moment of terrible insight into her own weak character, that Zoe could see she'd never meant for either Jess or his children to have a truly fair opportunity to like her or not. Somewhere in a love-starved, greedy part of her heart, she'd become so obsessed to win them over, that she'd aimed to do whatever it took.

Zoe glanced toward J.D., struggling to recover from her stark insights, intending to summon her lighthearted facade to arrange an escape. But the instant her gaze connected with the alert glimmer in his, she faltered. It was on the tip of her tongue to say something to prompt him to get them into lunch and away from Jess, but the glib words failed to come. To be so abruptly stripped of her sparkling veneer was horrifying. And the fact that J.D. was watching her so intently elevated her panic to unbearable proportions.

"I'd better let the two of you get on in to your meal," Jess said, unknowingly rescuing Zoe. "After I see to the kids, I'll be gettin' down the road. I'll give you a call from Ft. Worth," he said to J.D., then added, "And if those kids of mine cause any bother, you be sure to give them what for. Melanie's comin' out to stay with them nights, so let her know if there're any problems."

J.D. gave a brisk nod. "They'll be fine. Have a safe trip."

"Will do."

With that, Jess glanced at Zoe and touched a finger to his hat brim before he strode off in the direction of the garage.

Zoe turned to hurry for the back porch, desperate to find a few moments of privacy to compose herself. The tender violence of her feelings for her family were whirling like a cyclone, but the black truths about herself weighted her heart with despair.

How on earth could she face Jess Everdine now and tell him who she really was? What had ever made her think she could buy her way into his life, get his children to like her, then drop her awful bombshell? Why hadn't she simply written him a letter to introduce herself, then followed it up with a phone call? She would have at least demonstrated some regard for his wishes. Then she could have confessed that her secret search for her birth family had been found out, and the details—with names—would soon be published in the Sedgewick's unauthorized biography. Jess would have been shocked and possibly angry, but he and his children wouldn't have suffered the additional emotional complications Zoe would be perpetrating on them this way.

And all because of her twisted need to meet them first and win them over. The pitiful search little Spenser

Sedgewick had embarked upon all that time ago and doggedly pursued year after year to its fruitless conclusion had been devastating. It must have also damaged her judgment and her consideration for the feelings of others, she realized grimly.

The truth was, she'd never wanted to allow Jess a say in her determination to enter his children's lives. She'd simply vetoed his choice in the matter. Even buying into Hayes hadn't been quite the noble act she'd let herself think—not when becoming J.D.'s partner put Jess in a position that was subordinate to hers.

Suddenly the scope of her machinations seemed as breathtakingly vast as they were despicable.

Zoe entered the house and charged through the kitchen, headed for the refuge of the small bathroom down the hall. Once she shut herself in, she whipped off her Stetson, twisted on the cold water tap, then bent down. She repeatedly dashed her hot face with cool water, but was shaking so badly that water splattered everywhere. She was finally forced to stop and instead hold both wrists under the cascade as she waited for calm.

It was several minutes before she was able to return to the kitchen and sit down for lunch. By the time she did, the outward sparkle of Zoe Yahzoo was too blindingly bright to be anything but a poorly overacted performance.

Zoe didn't know if she'd survive the afternoon. Particularly when J.D. seemed determined to run her from one end of the ranch to the other. She'd resented having no time alone to sort out the mess she'd made and find some solution to fix it all. But by day's end she was grateful for the fatigue that had taken the razor edge off her anxieties. By the time they'd had a quiet supper and she'd gone upstairs to shower, the glum knowledge that she'd made a horrendous mistake that couldn't be fixed settled over her.

She'd continue on with her plan to spend time with her brother and sister, perhaps get to know them a bit, but she wouldn't go out of her way to win them over. As soon as Jess returned from Ft. Worth, she'd talk to him, confess what she'd done and offer to help in any way she could to minimize the fallout from the biography on Bobby and Becky. Though she feared there was little chance of that, at least Jess would have time to prepare them for what was coming.

Too restless for bed, Zoe dressed and went downstairs, hoping for a distraction from her gloomy mood. She wound up in the hall outside J.D.'s office. The door was open, so she stopped and knocked softly on the door frame.

That J.D. was in bad humor was evident by the surly look he leveled on her. "No early bedtime, Hollywood?"

Zoe shook her head and slipped her fingers into her front jeans' pockets. "Nope. That shower and fresh change of clothes perked me right up, J.D."

His dark eyes made a head-to-toe pass over her that made her smile. For all his crankiness, J.D. liked her. It was a perception that made her dare an attempt at friendship, but she didn't want to push him. The upsetting insights into her character and motivations that day made her more cautious about going out of her way to win anyone over. Even someone she liked as much as she liked J.D.

She shrugged. "Just thought I'd stop by and get a look at your office before I went in to watch TV or listen to some music." She hesitated. "If that's all right."

''Fine with me.'' He'd raised his hands to rest his fists on his hips and was simply watching her.

Zoe felt uneasy under his hard gaze. Her lighthearted ''Thanks'' and her quick turn to head down the hall was nothing less than a fast getaway. It was an enormous relief to escape the scrutiny of his dark gaze. Something in its intensity was a fresh reminder of the look he'd given her after she'd met Jess. J.D. was far too perceptive, and worse, he must have detected something then that had made him suspicious. She'd hoped their wearing afternoon together and the fact that she'd eventually recovered enough to behave with Zoe Yahzoo normalcy had made him forget. That he hadn't was plain.

Zoe took a quick detour upstairs for her CD case, then brought it back down to the living room. She set the case on a nearby table, then selected the first disc. Taking a moment to look over the stereo system, she put in the disc and wandered several steps away. In seconds, Led Zepplin's ''Whole Lotta Love'' erupted from the speakers.

Startled, Zoe raced back to the volume control and slid the lever to a much lower range. Her hope that J.D.— and Carmelita in her quarters on the east end of the house—hadn't been unduly alarmed faded the instant she turned and saw J.D. leaning against the side of the wide doorway, his arms crossed over his chest.

His ''What the hell is that?'' was so prickly, she smiled.

''Led Zepplin.'' Her answer made him cock his head as if he either couldn't hear her or hadn't understood. She reached over and popped out the disc. ''I take it you're not a fan,'' she said, then put in another disc. The Garth Brooks CD sent some lively country music through the speakers. ''Better?''

His low, "Much," and the way he uncrossed his arms and came toward her made her smile widen. He paused at her CD case and glanced over the eclectic mix of music from Bach to the Eagles, and Zoe noted with relief that some of his surliness eased.

She dared a soft, "Do you slow dance, John Dalton?" as the song neared its end. The next tune would start soon and its slow pace would be suitable.

J.D.'s head came up suddenly, the surprise that flickered in his dark eyes the tiniest moment shunted aside by a wariness that was macho male. Her hint for him to dance with her had evidently usurped what he might consider his male prerogative.

On the other hand, perhaps he wasn't used to women asking him to dance. It made Zoe wonder how many idiot females lived in this part of Texas.

His voice was stern. "Are you flirting with me, Hollywood?"

Zoe appeared to consider it, then nodded and said somberly, "Yeah, John Dalton, I think I am."

The shockwave of her admission hit his chest like a soft punch. She smiled another high-watt smile, but the look in her neon eyes was a beguiling mix of sincerity and anxiety. The idea that Zoe, for all her brash playfulness, might be a tad worried about how he'd respond, was another confirmation of the emotional vulnerability he kept sensing. It was also a flattering indication that there was something serious about her flirting with him.

Which made him wary as hell. His eyes narrowed. "Why?"

Zoe shrugged. "I guess I like you."

He gave a skeptical shake of his head and Zoe laughed softly. She fixed him with a glittering look, then stepped in front of him. Just that quickly, she placed one small hand on his shoulder and caught hold of his hand.

Unable to resist, J.D. slipped his free hand around her, then flexed his arm to pull her flush against him. Her eyes widened at his sudden forcefulness. J.D. glared down at her as the song ended, then waited several beats into the ballad that followed before he started them in the slow steps.

Zoe's breath caught. Everything about the man was a thrill, and everything feminine in her went into an uproar. She could barely breathe as he moved against her, leading her in the simple steps that forced the softness of her body against the warm hard abrasion of his.

She couldn't look away from the earthy sensuality that gave his rugged features a fierce cast. She'd never before been the object of such concentrated intensity from a man who was so blatantly male. Moving against him was like pressing into flames and she felt herself melt. The instinct to somehow wrap herself around him and never let go compelled her to pull her hand from his and reach up to encircle his neck. As her arms tightened around him, his arms tightened around her, bringing her soft cheek against the hard angle of his jaw.

Zoe pulled herself higher until her lips hovered close to his ear. She'd meant to make a frivolous remark, but her voice was a little too breathless to carry it off. "If you're trying to give me a thrill, John Dalton, you're succeeding."

He gave a rough chuckle, his warm breath gusting into her ear. "Are you amusing yourself at my expense, Goldilocks?" The harsh edge of his growled words was an unintentional revelation, and Zoe's heart swelled with tenderness. The idea that big, gruff John Dalton might have an emotional vulnerability or two touched her.

She snuggled tighter against him, her cheek pressed firmly to his. "I don't think so."

His low, "When will you know for sure?" made her laugh softly.

"I know right now that I like you," she admitted recklessly. "That I think you might be the most appealing man in Texas—perhaps the most appealing man I've ever met. I know I'd like to get to know you, I'd like to see if the attraction I feel toward you is mutual. And...if anything could come from it—"

At his disbelieving snort, she drew back and grinned up at him. "But if I said all that to you now, either you might not believe me, or you'd be scared off, so..." She paused to tap a finger on his lean cheek. "I think I'll stick with 'I don't think so,' and let you wonder."

J.D. swore and gave her another of his hard looks. "You're a hell of a flirt."

She grinned. "I've been practicing a long time while I waited to meet you, John Dalton."

As if her outrageous confessions had finally won him over, the long creases on one side of his face curved to his cheekbones in a half smile that was as cynical as it was amused.

"You could get yourself in a lot of trouble with talk like that."

Zoe's whispered, "Is that your personal guarantee?" as she snuggled her cheek against his jaw, drew a growled, "Ah, hell," from him, but his arms tightened to hold her in a pleasant crush that felt so heavenly that Zoe sighed.

Only dimly did she realize when the song ended. Eyes closed, she was so lost in the incredible security and sensual heat of him that she wasn't aware of much else.

Until the next song on the CD didn't start. Until the strange rigidity that swept J.D.'s body registered. The disappointment of being slowly released was indescribable. But it was nothing compared to being gently pushed away from all that male heat and opening dazed eyes to catch the harsh twist of J.D.'s mouth.

His low, "Song's over," was final. The way he turned to exit the room made it so.

Though Zoe slept well enough that night, she awoke the next morning edgy and bursting with nervous energy. Trying to eat breakfast while sitting across the table from a silent J.D. made her nervousness spike higher. Had he guessed that her flippant remarks about liking him were more serious than she'd made them sound?

As he worked steadily at clearing his plate, Zoe had the strong impression that he was sorting through his thoughts in much the same methodical, efficient way. That his thoughts were somehow centered on her was just as startling an impression. He was a rancher who should have had the workings of the vast Hayes Ranch on his mind, but there was something penetrating in his occasional glance, something personal that seemed to probe deeper into her with every stroke.

Unnerved, Zoe finally gave up on her meal. After a lifetime of successfully hiding her true feelings, the mere idea that J.D. might have x-ray vision into hers was disturbing.

She quickly got up and carried her dishes to the sink to rinse with water. Stepping out of his line of sight helped. "What do you have planned for us today, J.D.?" she asked.

He waited until she turned off the tap before he answered. "I'd planned for 'us' to go our separate ways."

The statement dealt a mild sting, but Zoe turned to give him a smile to cover it. "Tired of me already, huh? I thought you Texans were made of sterner stuff."

"We are," he answered, "but I was hoping to ask my partner for a favor."

Zoe was instantly intrigued. There was something nice about the way he'd said the words "my partner." And that was no mean feat for a man opposed to sharing a square inch of his birthright.

"A favor?" Her beaming smile was genuine. She would bet her trust fund that John Dalton Hayes rarely asked anyone for a favor. "A big favor, a small one— or are you joking?"

"I'd have to have a sense of humor to make jokes, Hollywood." He scraped his chair back and stood. "You can decide for yourself how big the favor is."

The way he delayed by pushing his chair up to the table and gathering his dishes to carry to the sink heightened Zoe's suspense. "So what's the favor?"

J.D. turned on the tap to rinse his hands as he answered. "Becky Everdine is trying to save money for college. I've hired her to paint the wood fence from the highway. It's a big job in the heat." As he dried his hands on a nearby towel, the half smile he gave her bore traces of the sense of humor he denied having. "Since you and I are co-owners and we both benefit from ranch improvements, you could give her a hand and our joint tenancy wouldn't have to pay a nickel more."

Zoe struggled to keep her smile in place and reveal nothing of the excitement that stormed over her at the prospect of working with her sister. The dread that followed was a reminder that she would be compounding her mistakes if she involved herself with Becky to that extent. Jess would be livid once he knew everything, but Zoe knew already that she'd risk it. "The two of you have already agreed on a price?"

"That's right."

Zoe's smile faded and she gave him a stern look. "You aren't paying her what would really amount to minimum wage, are you?"

J.D. shook his head to that. "I got a professional painter's bid before I offered the job to her. She's getting paid the going rate of the pros."

Zoe couldn't help the impulse to look out for the girl's interests. "Pros would do the job with a power sprayer."

A faint frown line deepened between J.D.'s brows. "No power sprayer. I don't want paint sprayed into pasture grass, so they'll have to be done by hand."

"She gets the same amount of money if I help?"

J.D. gave her a narrow look. "You're awfully worried about what she's getting paid."

Zoe shrugged. "Sometimes people take advantage of kids. They expect them to do adult work, but they don't want to pay adult wages."

His scowl was immediate. "I don't treat kids that way, Hollywood."

Zoe's smile and her, "I didn't think you would, but I had to ask," seemed to appease him.

He tilted his head back and looked down at her. "Have you ever painted anything besides your fingernails?" The gleam of amusement in his eyes was retaliation.

Zoe waved the question away and smiled. "How hard can it be?"

J.D.'s chuckle both delighted her and gave her the strong hint that there might be more to the job than she thought.

Zoe would ever be grateful for the case of sunblock she'd brought with her to Texas. Every square inch of skin not covered by her tank top, cut-off jeans and boots was liberally coated to thwart the harsh rays of the Texas sun. That she'd insisted Becky's young skin was also thickly coated amused Becky. When Zoe made them stop painting fence at almost eleven that morning so they could apply a fresh layer of sunblock, Becky groaned.

"We're going to run out of sunblock before we run out of paint," she teased, but dutifully uncapped the tube Zoe had given her earlier and squirted some into her palm. "It's a good thing we've got work gloves, or our hands would be too slippery with this gunk to hold the brushes."

Zoe sent her a mock glare. "Sermonette number four. Taking care of your skin is a high personal priority, young lady. You have a fabulous complexion, but if you don't protect it, everyone will be calling you saddle-face before you're twenty-five."

Becky laughed. "I'm not going to be a movie star or a model, Zoe."

Zoe shook her head. "Doesn't matter. Aside from health concerns, you have the looks and the brains to be anything you want. Why not take care of both and keep all your options?"

Becky shrugged to that, and Zoe was struck again by the familiarity of the gesture. Though Zoe privately admitted that she was vain enough to have spent significant time in front of mirrors checking her appearance, those times had acquainted her with a spectrum of her own natural expressions and gestures. That she'd witnessed several of them from Becky that morning was a bit staggering.

Were such things as biting the insides of your cheeks to keep from laughing, flipping a skein of hair behind an ear in a certain way, or setting your mouth just so when you worked at a detailed part of a task genetic? Were impish grins, wide-eyed, mock-horror faces and giggles engraved somewhere in DNA? Zoe had met her sister less than twenty-four hours before, but she'd seen enough that morning to convince her that it had to be.

Watching Becky as they worked facing each other from opposite sides of the board fence had been a lot like looking at herself in a mirror. Zoe was too fascinated by the whole idea to think of worrying about how strongly she and Becky resembled each other.

Until J.D. drove the pickup down the ranch drive to pick them up for lunch. He pulled over to their side of the drive and stopped the truck to call out, "Never underestimate the ability of females to get the job done."

Becky and Zoe automatically glanced down the fence line to the highway, noting that they'd painted almost half of the fence on that side of the drive. Their shared grin of accomplishment when they looked over the fence at each other was another mirror expression that jolted Zoe.

Nervousness had her looking away to bend down to tap the lid on her paint can and gather her rag and brushes. She took her time, giving Becky a chance to collect her own and slip through the unpainted section of fence next to them. She let Becky choose her own route through the shallow ditch, deliberately crossing it herself a few feet away.

Now that she was so acutely aware of the resemblance between her and her sister, she couldn't imagine how anyone else could see the two of them side by side and miss it. Eagle-eyed J.D. was sure to catch on, and she was suddenly terrified he'd figure out everything before she could talk to Jess. Without a word, she hefted her empty cans into the truck bed. As Becky did the same, Zoe was relieved that J.D. was staring out the windshield. Becky waited for her on the passenger side of the pickup, but Zoe waved at her to get into the truck first. She figured she didn't need the added flurry of nerves that would come from sitting next to J.D.

"Nice job, ladies," J.D. remarked, putting the pickup into gear to make a turn in the wide drive.

"Thanks," Becky said, "but you can drop me off at home. Bobby's already there."

"Do you kids want to eat at the main house?" he asked.

"I made lunch ahead and I've got to get the laundry done this afternoon before we start on the fences after four. Besides, I need to shower off all this sunblock." Becky turned her head to send Zoe a sparkling look that made Zoe smile. "Don't be surprised if we slide off the seats."

J.D. chuckled and started the pickup down the drive toward the foreman's house. They let Becky out moments later, and Zoe climbed back in the pickup, adjusting the air-conditioning vents to hit her flushed face. When she'd stepped out of the truck to let Becky out, she'd happened to catch the sharp look J.D. gave them as they stood together briefly. Though she now stared straight ahead, she could feel the touch of J.D.'s gaze whenever he glanced her way.

"You and Becky look enough alike to be cousins," he drawled.

The alarm that shot through Zoe nearly stopped her heart. Her shaky, "Is that right?" was so flimsy that she winced.

His casual, "That's a fact," bore a thread of purpose that Zoe was alert to. She resisted the urge to look over at him to confirm it. His much softer, "Or sisters," suddenly made her light-headed with distress.

She somehow got in enough air to give a light laugh. "My roommate one year at boarding school was a blonde. Given my father's reputation, there was constant speculation that we were half-sisters. She was shorter, thinner and wore glasses. We finally decided that because we were blue-eyed blondes, people didn't really look past our coloring to see the differences."

Zoe said no more, scooting forward on the bench seat to pull her tube of sunblock from her back pocket, hoping the casual movement would be a distraction.

That it didn't distract J.D. was evident in his faintly skeptical, "Uh-huh," before he eased the pickup to a stop under a shade tree near the house.

Several times in those next two days, Zoe was tempted to acknowledge the undercurrent of speculation in J.D. and try out her revelations on him. She chickened out every time. Meanwhile, she and Becky worked like fiends mornings and late afternoons until almost dark, finishing the fences two days later. It pleased Zoe that Becky had asked if she could come to the big house for makeup tips some evening. She'd even got to spend some time with Bobby when he'd invited her to see his progress on the tree house and took her to a nearby creek to look for frogs.

Zoe came to the not-so-surprising conclusion that her brother and sister were the two most lovable and fun kids on the planet. That they both seemed to like her was an enormous relief.

And that increased her sense of doom. Jess would return home in two more days, and what she'd have to tell him could get her banished from Bobby and Becky's lives. Once their names and their location on the Hayes Ranch was published, the media would all but parachute into their front yard for photos and interviews. Their mother's premarital indiscretion would become common knowledge, and their memories of her would be tarnished. That they might suffer the ridicule of their classmates was another torment for Zoe, a dark confirmation that her existence would bring no more joy to her biological family than it had to her adoptive one.

Zoe's mood swung low, but she kept it carefully hidden behind bright smiles and unflagging good humor. Once the painting was finished, she was J.D.'s shadow, teasing him, working at his side, fairly beaming with Zoe Yahzoo brilliance. J.D.'s men seemed to like her, and her twice-a-day raids on Coley's homemade ice cream were always attended by Becky and Bobby, with more of J.D.'s men joining in each time, until J.D. complained his cowhands were likely to put on more weight before fall than his cattle.

But no matter how lively and fun she was, none of it was enough to completely remove the speculation that shone in J.D.'s dark gaze from time to time. In spite of her worries about that, Zoe enjoyed playing a bright counterpart to his prickly moods and gray humor. That she was able to tease a real smile or a gravelly chuckle from him was fast becoming the highlight of her day.

What she'd sensed from the first—that she could easily fall in love with John Dalton Hayes—was rapidly becoming a real possibility. Not even the dismal knowledge that she possessed some mysterious flaw that kept others from loving her back was enough to thwart her increasing affection for him.

CHAPTER FIVE

"Is SOMETHING wrong, Carmelita?"

Zoe had just stepped into the kitchen from the back door to the loud sounds of Carmelita banging pots and pans together as she unloaded the dishwasher. Carmelita's angry scowl and her muttered words, which were probably as close to swearing as she ever came, surprised Zoe.

"*Señora*?" Zoe hung her hat on a wall peg as she waited for the woman to hear her over the din and notice she'd come in.

Carmelita swung toward her, the large skillet in her hand unintentionally threatening. Zoe's grin seemed to interrupt the Mexican woman's tirade long enough for her to realize she held the big skillet like a club. Flustered, she lowered it and bent to shove it in a low cupboard.

Zoe tried again. "Is something wrong, *señora*?"

The Mexican woman nodded, and a new flush of anger surged up her cheeks. The spate of rapid Spanish that followed was so swift that Zoe could only pick out and translate two words. But those two—heifer and Boss—combined with Carmelita's obvious outrage to hint that her upset had to do with J.D. and his ex-wife.

When Carmelita paused to take a breath, Zoe interjected, "Is J.D. upset?"

Which set off a whole new tirade, complete with dramatic arm waves and a new attack on the hapless pots and pans in the dishwasher. Zoe nodded seriously, as if she understood every word, then carefully stepped around Carmelita toward the refrigerator.

She quickly opened the door, snagged two bottles of J.D.'s beer, then turned toward Carmelita and held them up. Carmelita continued on with her rapid-fire Spanish, but nodded and jerked her head in the direction of J.D.'s den.

Zoe popped the lids off on the bottle opener, then started for the hall and made her way to J.D.'s private lair. The door was standing open, but Zoe hesitated to catch sight of J.D. and try to gage his reception to her intrusion.

He was slumped on the leather couch along one wall, his head back against the cushions, his eyes closed. Zoe stepped into the room and his lashes opened a slit, then squeezed closed in obvious irritation.

"You look like you might be in the mood for a beer and some sympathy, Pilgrim."

J.D. raised a wide hand and ran it down his face before he let it fall to his chest. "Don't you ever run low on energy and Pollyanna cheer?" he muttered darkly.

Unfazed by his surly manner, Zoe dropped down next to him on the sofa and passed him the sweating longneck when he opened his eyes. He took the bottle with clear reluctance, but put it to his mouth and swallowed nearly half the contents before he set it aside.

"What're you doin' in here? Did Coley run out of ice cream early?" he grumbled, then eased his head back on the cushion to glare at her. It was a look that never failed to intimidate anyone else.

The smile she gave him was so bright, he couldn't keep a corner of his mouth from quirking.

"It's not so early, J.D." Zoe took a quick sip of her beer, then grimaced at the taste. "How do you stand this stuff?" She shoved it in his direction and he took it. Zoe turned more fully toward him and braced her elbow on the back of the sofa to give him a long, thoughtful look. The fact that she said nothing for several moments aggravated him.

"What is it you came in here for?" he groused.

"First, to find out what happened. Carmelita explained everything, but she was talking at warp speed and my Spanish is a little faulty." She gave him a wry smile. "Something about the Boss and a heifer. I guessed she wasn't talking about the cattle, so I figured she was talking about your ex-wife."

His eyes narrowed. "That's a sore subject."

Zoe nodded and said, "No doubt," before she went on. "The other reason I came in was to assess the damage and see if I could cheer you up and help you recapture the optimistic world view you're so well known for." She grinned when he snickered. "Partners ought to do that for each other, you know."

"Ah, hell," he growled on an outrush of bad temper, and closed his eyes. "Go find your wings, Tinkerbell, and fly on outta here."

"So you'd rather pine after Raylene in private, huh?" she persisted. When his eyes flew open and he fixed her with a sour look, she reached over and gave his arm a pat. "I get the message."

For J.D., that little hit-and-run touch was one too many. He reflexively caught her hand as she pulled it away. "What did you really come in here for?"

Zoe pulled her elbow from the back of the sofa and leaned her shoulder against it, her expression sobering as she looked down at the firm grip he had on her hand. An instant later she was looking him straight in the eye, her lips on the verge of another megawatt smile. "To flirt a little and see if I could take advantage of you. What else? I've heard all about men on the rebound.''

''What did I tell you about talk like that?'' he grumbled.

Zoe gave a shrug. ''That I could get into a lot of trouble,'' she answered softly. ''But so far, it looks like you Texans are all talk.''

The gauntlet was down. The few inches between them fairly crackled with sensuality. Zoe couldn't breathe as she kept her gaze locked firmly with the sudden intensity in J.D.'s.

His gravelly drawl was deadly serious. ''This is a bad idea, Hollywood.''

Zoe's voice was just as serious. ''I have lots of bad ideas, John Dalton.'' She leaned so close to his lips that he felt the soft gust of her breath as she added, ''This is probably the only one I won't regret acting on.'' She let her mouth drift just close enough to touch his, then stopped, the sudden agony she felt when J.D. didn't respond tearing through her like razors.

His lips chafed against hers as he whispered roughly, ''What's the matter, darlin'? Lose your nerve?''

In that incredible moment, Zoe knew she had. For all she'd sensed of the high-voltage sensuality between them, her strong belief in being ultimately rejected by anyone important to her was clamoring for her to retreat. Nothing less than the terror of adding J.D. to that list could have given her the will to back off.

In a flash, Zoe was off the sofa, the unexpected yank of her hand breaking J.D.'s light grip.

But if she'd thought to make a fast getaway, she was mistaken. J.D.'s long arm whipped out and he seized her other wrist before she could take a step. Alarmed, Zoe looked down into eyes so dark with purpose that her knees went weak. Time seemed to slow as he towed her toward him. As if he had all the time in the world, J.D. controlled her descent, maneuvering her until she was flat on her back beneath him on the sofa. Keeping his dark eyes locked with the faint apprehension in hers, his head came down at the same relentless pace.

At the last second, Zoe's lashes drifted closed and his mouth covered hers, his tongue shoving past her lips to work with shattering expertise. Zoe could barely get enough air as she allowed J.D. access. His kiss was blatantly carnal, worthy of his overwhelming maleness. His heavy weight pressed down on her, satisfying a craving she'd been unaware she possessed.

Joy pulsed through her veins, a dizzying counterpart to the heavy beat of arousal that thundered through her body. She suddenly knew she loved this gruff, harsh man, and would to the end of her days. He was real and solid, a man of the land. He was settled and enduring, and the security she'd hungered for her whole life was such a natural by-product of who he was that he was irresistible.

I have so little to offer a man like him. The despairing thought made her clutch at him, as if she could forget her flaws and meld with his solid essence while there was still time. But she was a bit of fluff to a man like him, shallow, unprincipled and selfish. Soon, he'd know it all. In the light of his strongly defined character and down-to-earth life-style, she was a flighty fake, too given to impulse to have put down roots, too unsure of herself to be reliable.

The bleak despair she'd lived with all her life welled up. Loath to let it mix with the passion thudding through her, she turned her head and broke off the kiss. She clung to him tightly, both to get control of her pain and to hoard the wonderful feel of him.

J.D. was certain he'd lost his mind. He never should have caught her, never should have compelled her to make a payment on all her little flirtations. Hadn't he learned anything? The last fancy little blonde he'd fallen for had made a jackass of him. This fancy little blonde, Hollywood-bright and irrepressible, had the potential to leave him bare-assed in a cold wind.

J.D. slowly lifted his head. He looked down harshly into neon eyes shiny with emotion and suddenly knew he couldn't be cruel. It was a grim fact that he already liked Zoe too much.

So, he settled for silence. He was stunned that it was so hard to ease himself off her delectably curved little body, shocked that turning his back on her and leaving the room could give him such an ache.

Zoe felt the terrible impact of J.D.'s silence as it underscored and confirmed her innermost beliefs about herself. She didn't speak, either, could only watch as he pulled back and she let him go. A chill settled over her without the heat of him. The chill pierced her heart as he walked from the room and she heard his heavy step retreat down the hall and eventually go up the stairs. She lay a long time in the awful silence of the room before she got up and made her way to her own room.

The fact that Zoe sat across from him at breakfast that next morning, as cheery and playful as ever, knotted J.D.'s gut with guilt. He knew his abandonment the night before had hurt her; he'd seen it in those remarkable neon eyes. That she was treating him to the full Zoe Yahzoo persona was a sure indication that the hurt lingered.

J.D. didn't understand why he knew that, or why he cared so much. He sure as hell hadn't been this perceptive with anyone else, Raylene included. But there was something about Zoe that got to him, something about her that sent out signals he could decode. A lot was going on beneath her sparkle and fun, and hurt over his abrupt withdrawal the night before was just part of it.

J.D.'s mood darkened at the reminder. Zoe's intrusion into his life was much more significant than the self-indulgent cowgirl whims of a rich socialite. He'd got an inkling of that when she'd met the Everdines. He'd found out later from movie buff Carmelita that Zoe was the *adopted* daughter of the Sedgewicks.

So, when he'd seen the uncanny resemblance between Zoe and Becky the day they started painting the fence, the truth had hit him like a lightning bolt. He'd been disappointed in Zoe when she'd rebuffed his remarks about the resemblance, but if his suspicions about why she was here were correct, that made Zoe Yahzoo one of the most dishonest and manipulative people he'd ever met.

So why couldn't he judge her as harshly as she deserved? Why did he care that he'd hurt her feelings the night before?

J.D.'s dark mood faltered. It was precisely because there was something about Zoe that got to him. There was something lost and a little broken underneath that Tinkerbell facade, something so melancholy and unsure that there was no way he could bring himself to crush it.

Jess Everdine might not feel the same way. Which landed J.D. squarely between a trusted and respected friend, and a deceitful little partner who'd brought sparkle to his life and had awakened a tenderness in him he hadn't known existed.

It took a surprising amount of energy to be Zoe Yahzoo that morning at the breakfast table. Nonchalance was the best choice, both for her and for J.D. There was no point in making the man feel bad because she wasn't his cup of tea. There was certainly no point in acting hurt and making him leery of spending time with her. Zoe knew herself well enough to know that she'd probably still flirt, still hope for J.D. to return some of her feelings for him. Anything long-term with him was doomed, of course, but Zoe realized that she would rather have a little with J.D. for a short time, than make herself do without entirely.

When this was over, she'd go someplace else, patch herself up and find something to do. She still had her little hideaway ranch in California and her house in the Hollywood Hills. There were plenty of charities and causes that might still want her patronage after the biography was published. Then again, she could write a new screenplay. The first two had sold, but had not yet been produced. She had several more ideas. Immersing herself in those—in anything—would likely once again rescue her emotionally.

It was in the midst of reviewing her options for a life after she left the Hayes Ranch, that Zoe fully realized how strongly she believed in her capacity to fail with the Everdines and to have any possibility with J.D. jinxed. Common sense told her no one could be so profoundly hopeless when it came to finding love. Experience had given her a much more dismal expectation on the subject.

So, Zoe smiled and bantered her way through breakfast with J.D. She'd wait out the last two days before Jess's return, selfishly take as much as she was allowed with Bobby and Becky, grab whatever she could with J.D. After she talked to Jess, she'd weather what he dished out, then endure J.D.'s choler when she told him about the biography and the trouble she expected it to bring to the Hayes Ranch.

But the really tragic part of it all, was that none of the animosity she would endure could spare young Bobby and Becky a particle of the hurt and upset she was bringing into their lives. No level of immersion into a life after Hayes would ever lessen her guilt and regret on that score.

"Is Bobby doing what I think he is?" Zoe squinted toward the shaded end of the barn as she and Becky rode back to the ranch headquarters. The late morning heat beat down on them from a Texas sun that was now blindingly bright. They'd been checking fences all morning, and Zoe was relieved at the prospect of the noon break.

Bobby, however, was throwing some good-size rocks toward the apex of the stable roof. That could only mean that he'd spied the wasp nest up there and was engaged in the boy-child sport of stirring up trouble.

Becky's exasperated sigh was answer enough as she glanced in Bobby's direction. She abruptly neck-reined her horse and turned off. "I'm going to the other door. If he knocks that one down, I don't want to be anywhere near that side of the barn when it falls. You coming?"

Zoe glanced toward Bobby, then looked over at Becky and shook her head. "You aren't going to stop him?" She couldn't help but be surprised. She thought that occasionally pulling rank on a younger sibling was a big sister's prerogative.

Becky rolled her eyes. "What for? He wouldn't stop anyway, unless the wasps sting him. Or J.D. catches him at it." Becky grinned at that.

Zoe looked back to see Bobby getting ready to pitch another rock, not able to be as pragmatic. Everything she'd ever heard about bee sting allergies made her worry for Bobby. The Hayes Ranch was a long way from trauma level medical attention. "Has he ever been stung before?"

"Nah, and that's the problem. If he ever got stung good, he'd probably quit." Becky paused. "On the other hand, he's so ornery, he'd probably do it again anyway. Are you coming this way, or are you going to take your chances with the wasps?"

Zoe waved her away. "You go ahead. I think I'll see if I can warn him off."

Becky rode in the other direction, her light laugh letting Zoe know what she thought of Zoe's chances.

Zoe rode on a few more feet, then dismounted to go the rest of the short distance on foot. Bobby's back was toward her, and he seemed so absorbed in perfecting his aim that he didn't hear her approach.

Zoe stopped directly behind him, waited until he pitched another rock, then gave him a light tickle on the ribs. Her stern, "What are you doing, young man?" timed with the tickle, made the boy jump in guilty surprise.

The next moment the wasp nest hurtled downward, landing with a thump in the dust not two feet in front of them. Bobby reacted automatically, vaulting out of harm's way to successfully escape the outraged wasps.

Stunned, Zoe's gaze dropped in disbelief to home in on the downed nest. Before she could move, the wasps swarmed her, their mad buzzing as unnerving as the occasional tap when one flew against her hat or her clothes. Zoe froze, hoping her lack of movement wouldn't further agitate the wasps and give them a target. But they were too riled to ignore her. Zoe gasped as she felt the first sting, then several others.

A second later J.D. came barreling out of the stable, a can of wasp repellant in hand. In one sweep, the fog from the repellant misted the air in front of her from her shoulders to her feet before it was aimed at the downed nest. Zoe bolted for the shade of the stable, not stopping until she came to a halt at the far end. She barely had time to assess the damage when she heard J.D.'s shout and the reassuring sound of him running after her.

"Did you get stung?" Suddenly he was in front of her, concern drawing his dark brows together as he looked her over.

"Yeah, I think I did," she answered, managing an offhand tone as she glanced down at the places that throbbed with an odd sensation of numbness and sharp pain. Because she still felt as if she were still being stung, it was a surprise to see there were no wasps attached to her shirt and jeans.

Bobby came tearing up and halted anxiously at her side. "You got stung? I'm sorry, Zoe." The remorse in the boy's voice got her instant attention. "I'm sorry."

Zoe gave him a crooked smile and reached over to nudge the brim of his hat. "No harm done, squirt," she said, then leaned down into his face to add with playful menace, "Outside of *agonizing* pain. No more bee-baiting from you—ever—okay?"

Bobby's face was pale. "No, ma'am, I swear. I'll never bother bees or wasps again."

Zoe gave him a narrow look. "Not hornets, either, right?"

"Never, Miss Zoe. Nothing that stings, cross my heart." The childish vow and the accompanying X he drew on his chest was charmingly earnest.

Zoe straightened stiffly and patted his shoulder. "Good enough. How about getting Brute and putting him up for me?"

Bobby looked at J.D., but whether for permission or because he was expecting some sort of punishment, Zoe couldn't tell. Nevertheless, she intervened with a look that warned J.D. not to add to her mild reproof.

J.D. responded to it with a gruff, "Go ahead, Bobby. And keep your promise."

Bobby nodded animatedly. "Yessir, Mr. Hayes. I will." With that, the boy ran down the stable aisle just as Becky led her horse through the door behind J.D.

Zoe was too miserable with the sharply smarting wasp stings to have any questions from Becky delay her from getting to the house. She stepped briskly around J.D. and called a cheery, "See you later, Becky," as she left the stable for the house. J.D. was beside her in an instant.

"What about those stings?"

"Can't see or do much until we get to the house, J.D.," she noted with forced lightness. "I think I'll need Carmelita's help."

"Carmelita leaves lunch in the oven on Thursdays so she can do the shopping for the week."

Zoe chuckled and sent him a look. "Watch out, John Dalton. This situation just became rife with possibilities." In case he didn't catch her meaning, she wiggled her eyebrows.

J.D. glared over at her and gingerly took her arm to hurry her to the back sidewalk. "Why the hell do you do that?"

"What?"

"That whole damned I'm-gonna-make-a-joke-out-of-this-if-it-kills-me act?"

"So what would be better, bursting into tears and screaming that getting stung by a half dozen wasps hurts like a son of a b?" She grinned at his surprise over her near profanity. "Not my style, John Dalton."

Zoe ignored his gruff, "Hell," to that as they reached the porch steps. The wasp stings felt sharper with every step and she was eager to get inside.

They'd no more than got into the kitchen before the insistent pain had her tearing at her shirt buttons. The snap and zipper on her jeans were next. She spared J.D. a brief glance and quipped, "If you can't stand the heat, get out of the kitchen." With no more warning than that, she carefully plucked the front of her shirt away from her skin and peeled it off. She lowered her jeans next, wincing as the cloth chafed the stings on her thighs. She'd turned the denim fabric out to prevent any remaining stingers from nicking fresh skin, then stopped abruptly when she got them down as far as her knees.

"Uh-oh, John Dalton." She glanced up and gave him a pained smile. "Can you help me get my boots off?"

J.D. was too stunned by Zoe's sudden disrobing to react fast enough to exit the kitchen. Now that he could see the size of the welts across her middle and on her thighs, he was glad he hadn't. The misery that gave her eyes a suspicious sheen made him act immediately.

"Did you get any stings on your backside?" At her soft no, he cautiously reached for her. "Then I'll lift you to the counter."

Zoe straightened stiffly, and he slid his big hands under her arms to quickly lift her. He muttered over the snug fit of her small boots, but he got them off. He realized with some surprise that his hands actually shook when he dispensed with her jeans.

"You got allergies?" he asked as he carefully inspected the welts for any stingers he could see. Zoe's skin was like warm satin, its texture so delicate that his hands felt like huge patches of sandpaper.

Zoe looked down at J.D.'s bent head and smiled to herself as she gently removed his Stetson and set it aside. For all her brashness with him, her cheeks were on fire with embarrassment. It was one thing to flirt, but Zoe always avoided real intimacy. To sit on a kitchen cupboard in nothing but her bra and panties with a man like J.D. giving her nearly naked body his undivided attention was disconcerting. It also ranked as the most physically and emotionally intimate event of her life.

J.D. finished examining the welts and looked up into her flushed face. "I asked if you've got allergies. Ever been stung before?"

"I've been stung before, but not by wasps and not this many times. I got red and sore around the sting, but no big allergic reaction."

"We'll go see the doctor anyway," he decreed.

To Zoe's astonishment, J.D. plucked her off the counter to settle her in his arms and carry her across the kitchen. She automatically wrapped her arms around his neck.

"I can walk, John Dalton." In spite of the smarting stings, she couldn't help grinning at him. "And I probably don't need to see a doctor."

"We'll let the doctor decide whether you need to see him or not," he answered as they reached the stairs and started up. "Find something loose to put on while I call ahead to make sure they're ready for you."

Zoe laughed. "Do you think that's possible?"

J.D. hesitated at her door to give her a glare. His stony facade was cracking the tiniest bit and Zoe loved to see it. "No. I doubt I *could* prepare them for the full effect of a Zoe Yahzoo." He stepped through the door and gently stood her on her feet. For a handful of pulse-pounding moments, J.D.'s dark eyes probed into hers with a tenderness that stole her breath. "No one prepared me, but I'm finding out the surprise is part of the fun."

A second later his head lowered and he delivered a swift, hard kiss. "Get some clothes on." Just that suddenly, he turned and exited the room.

Zoe swayed on her feet, so surprised she forgot for a moment that she was standing in her underwear with a scattering of painful stings down the front of her.

I'm finding out the surprise is part of the fun. The words made her heart flutter wildly and, despite the stings, she practically flew to the armoire and riffled through the hanging clothes to find something loose-fitting—and attractive—to wear to town. She grabbed fresh underwear from a drawer and dashed to the bathroom for a quick shower. Moments later, she emerged, the lukewarm water aggravating the sting sites enough that even the soft flowing cotton of the pink sundress bothered them.

She got her sandals on and switched some of the contents from her purse into a small handbag that matched the sandals before J.D. returned. He came purposely toward her, but she held up a hand to ward him off.

"I need to walk, J.D." She demonstrated why as she held the sundress fabric away from the front of her. J.D.

took her handbag instead, then escorted her down the
stairs and out to the front of the house to where his big
car sat idling.

By the time they left the doctor's office after two o'clock,
Zoe was feeling much better, thanks to a sample tube of
topical cream the doctor had given her. They made a
quick trip to the pharmacy down the street to pick up
an over-the-counter antihistamine and fill a prescription
for more of the cream.

On their way home, J.D. stopped at the diner along
the highway to treat her to a late lunch. They returned
to the ranch sometime after three. J.D. pulled his car to
a stop behind the big station wagon Carmelita used,
which was now parked at the end of the back walk.

Zoe remembered then that she'd not collected her dis-
carded boots and clothes from where she'd taken them
off in the kitchen. She glanced over at J.D.'s profile.
"You didn't happen to pick up my clothes, did you?"
Her question brought J.D.'s head around.

His soft, "Hell," combined with the faint chagrin that
drew one corner of his mouth into a sheepish quirk, made
Zoe laugh.

She reached for her door handle and levered it open
to get out before J.D. could come around and chivalrously open it for her. She sent him a sparkling look
over the top of the car.

J.D. caught the look and pointed at her as if he were
leveling a gun. "Don't you dare."

Zoe grinned. "Why not?"

"Carmelita's awfully straight-laced."

Zoe burst out laughing. "And J.D. Hayes is the pin-
up boy for the adage, 'All work and no play.' Believe

me, J.D., Carmelita won't object to the idea that you've gone Texas bad.''

J.D. gave an emphatic shake of his head. "Carmelita will beat me black and blue with a skillet if she thinks I ravaged you in her kitchen the first time she left the house on an errand.''

Zoe walked around the front of J.D.'s car, her bright smile wide and playful. "Now how could you know how Carmelita will react, John Dalton? Was the kitchen a favorite ravaging place of yours when you were married?''

The question blunted J.D.'s expression. "It sure as hell was *not*—"

Zoe held up her hand to interrupt. "Let me guess—your wife was an aspiring actress, right? She was probably into moods and techniques, but with a particular fondness for artsy scenes in a *boudoir* with lacy costumes and scented candles. Nothing spur-of-the-moment or just-in-from-a-hard-day's-work for her, huh?''

J.D. glared down at her. "You've got a hell of a nerve, Zoe Yahzoo.''

Zoe grinned up into his formidable countenance. "I certainly do, John Dalton Hayes. And do you know what else?''

He muttered what had to be a swear word before he gave in to the inevitable. "What?''

Zoe reached over and touched his arm. "I'm glad she's not around anymore.''

Something softened the tiniest bit in J.D.'s hard expression. Zoe looked up somberly into his face. "And do you know what else?''

J.D. softened a little more. His voice was a gravelly whisper as he looked down at her. "What else?''

"I think I might like kitchens."

Zoe flitted away almost before she finished the outrageous remark, leaving J.D. to follow her to the back porch door. Zoe didn't wait for him to open it for her, but breezed in ahead of him, calling out a cheery hello to Carmelita.

"Are you all right, *señorita*?" Carmelita's face was the picture of concern as she looked Zoe over.

"I'm fine, *señora*. I forgot about leaving my clothes in the way. My apologies."

Carmelita's dark eyes went round. "*Sí*, I had questions when I found them." She looked past Zoe to J.D. to give him a stern look. "*Many* questions." Her attention returned to Zoe. "But Bobby and Becky came to help me carry things in and told me what happened."

Zoe nodded and grinned. "That's good. By the time we realized we'd dashed off too quick to pick them up, J.D. was pretty worried. He had visions of being whacked with a skillet."

Carmelita chuckled at that. "*Sí*. You are a young, unmarried woman. He is an experienced man. There is much between the two of you that needs a close watch."

"Ah, Carmelita." Zoe stepped over and gave the woman as good a hug as she could considering the stings. "Thank you for keeping watch over my virtue." She drew back and said in a loud whisper, "But it's really J.D. you need to protect."

J.D. finally spoke up. "That's no lie, Carmelita. This woman is the most shameless flirt I've ever met."

Carmelita wagged a finger at him. "And that is good for you, *señor*. You need a woman who flirts with you and makes you laugh." She then gave J.D. as stern a look as J.D. had ever seen. "And you need to marry such a woman and have many *niños* by her."

Zoe's breath caught at Carmelita's blunt advice. Her gaze streaked to J.D. in time to see his mildly amused expression ebb.

"Tried that once, didn't work out."

Carmelita shook her head to that. "That woman was a fortune digger who wanted your money. She did not want a home and a good man and many children." She turned her head to smile at Zoe. "This one has more money than you, a good heart and love for you in her eyes." She punctuated that with an affectionate pat on Zoe's cheek.

Zoe was so stunned by Carmelita's candor and unqualified endorsement or her suitability for J.D. that she couldn't speak.

As if the housekeeper knew the magnitude of the shock she'd dealt them both, she gave J.D. an admonishing glare, then turned to exit the room and go in the direction of her quarters on the east end of the house.

The heavy silence of the ranch kitchen wrapped around them both. Zoe held her breath, terrified J.D. would say something to spurn Carmelita's advice. She could only stare over into his lethally grim expression with round eyes as she waited for him to speak.

"Well, hell, Zoe," he said at last. "Now you've added *my* housekeeper to the Texas chapter of the Yahzoo fan club."

It took Zoe a moment to decide whether J.D.'s surly remark was meant to be humorous or not. She gave him a hesitant smile and dared a cheeky, "I'm still looking for a club president, John Dalton. Interested?"

J.D. reached up and gave his hat brim an irritable yank. "You stay in out of the heat this afternoon," he ordered gruffly before he turned toward the door. He wrenched it open, paused, then glanced back at her.

"And be sure to play some of that Lead Balloon rock music for Carmelita while you're at it."

He shut the door firmly behind him, leaving Zoe to sag against the nearest counter in profound relief.

CHAPTER SIX

ZOE went upstairs to change into a brief pair of cut-off jeans and a cotton shirt. The shorts ended above the stings and tying the tails of the shirt above her midriff would keep the other stings uncovered. Zoe decided to forego ice applications. The welts were less red and swollen already, giving her hope that she could return to normal activity the next day.

Drowsy from the antihistamine, she wandered downstairs and found the TV remote before she lounged on the sofa to scan the channels. She eventually settled on a national news channel, then tugged a nearby afghan over her for warmth against the air-conditioning, bending her knees to tent the fabric over the welts. She drifted into a nap soon after, and awakened later on her side, the afghan still over her.

The entertainment segment of the news channel came on and Zoe focused sleepily on it as she moved into a sitting position. She was trying to locate the remote to adjust the sound when a film excerpt of Jason and Angela Sedgewick came on.

Zoe's heart clenched at the unexpected feature, the surprise jolting her fully awake. She watched tensely as a montage of selective clips crossed the screen, the half dozen showing the Sedgewicks in some of their most volatile roles—from their vituperative exchange in *The Thorn*, to their Oscar-winning roles as maliciously clever schemers in *Wicked Ways*.

The reporter's story was to the point. "According to the unauthorized biography by Dillon Casey, the off-screen performances of the Sedgewicks bear close resemblance to some of their darkest and most critically acclaimed roles. From alleged infidelities of both during their twenty-five year marriage, their purported make-or-destroy influence over more than one actor's film career, to their alleged emotional abandonment of the daughter they adopted, Dillon Casey's tell-all book promises to be one of the most shocking revelations of the private lives of Hollywood greats ever written."

The segment went to a commercial and Zoe frantically made a new search for the remote. She finally found it on the floor just under the edge of the sofa, then switched it off. She sank back against the cushions as a huge wave of dread swept her.

News coverage had started—a full two weeks before she'd anticipated. Other than local newscasts and the small area newspaper, she hadn't watched or read much news since she'd got to Hayes, so it was possible coverage had begun days ago. And that meant every weekly magazine from *Newsweek* to the rags might be running articles. If any of them mentioned Bobby and Becky by name or gave away their location on the Hayes Ranch...

The thought sent Zoe springing from the sofa and hurriedly refolding the afghan. They'd been in the local pharmacy that afternoon and it hadn't occurred to her to check the magazine rack. The idea that the small towns nearby might already be saturated with news of the Sedgewicks sent her charging upstairs to change her clothes.

Mindless of the stings, Zoe tore through the armoire, trying to decide what to wear for a fast trip to town. If the story had already been published, she might be able to buy up every magazine copy and prevent it from being circulated in the area.

A new thought brought her to a sickening halt. Jess Everdine was in Ft. Worth. Whatever he was doing there, it would be unreasonable to expect that he wouldn't catch a newscast, read a newspaper or happen to pass a magazine rack. Her anxiety shot higher. It hadn't occurred to her to worry overmuch that his trip had delayed her from talking to him. What she had to tell him—particularly after her colossal manipulations to secretly enter his children's lives—was bad enough. If he discovered it all on his own from a premature news release, which might mention the kids' names or the Hayes Ranch, his reaction would be far worse.

Zoe swayed a moment, then grabbed a pair of jeans to go with the chambray shirt she'd selected. She made it to the bed before her shaking knees gave out. She sat several moments on the edge of the mattress as she fought to calm herself.

It hurt to realize that Jason and Angela had probably known about the early news releases for days. It was certain they'd have every article already published on the subject, as well as news videos. The fact that they hadn't bothered to warn her was further evidence that the breach between them had widened to unforgivable proportions.

Glumly, Zoe stood up just long enough to slide off her cutoffs, fling them aside, and sit back down to put on the jeans. She couldn't help that several former household employees of the Sedgewicks had consented to be interviewed by Dillon Casey as he'd researched his book. That they'd chosen to tell him the unpleasant details about the famous actors' relationship with their daughter hadn't been Zoe's fault, either. Not even the fact that Zoe herself had repeatedly spurned Casey's attempts to interview her had pleased Jason and Angela—not when they expected her to debunk the negative reports.

Zoe worked her jeans up enough to stand and tug them past the stings. In the end, she'd finally arranged to meet with Casey, but only because she'd learned that he'd found out about Bobby and Becky.

The meeting had been a nightmare. Casey had been ruthless in his efforts to get her to confirm or deny the information he'd gleaned during his research. Because she'd declined to comply, her straightforward plea that he not publish the kids' names and their location had fallen on deaf ears.

Dillon Casey wasn't intimidated by threats of lawsuits, wasn't persuaded by bribes. Jason and Angela had learned that. Zoe had learned that Dillon Casey had a rotten little black cinder where his heart should be.

She finished dressing, then went to the dresser. She took her wallet from her purse, then slid it in her pocket. If she hurried, she might be able to get to town, raid every magazine rack she could find, and be back in time for ice cream at the cook house.

She rushed downstairs, breezed through the kitchen and delivered a swift, "I won't be back until after supper, *señora*. I can make a cold snack out of what's left," and was out the door before Carmelita could do more than send her a surprised glance.

Moments later she'd got her car out and was on her way down the drive to the highway. She made the trip to town in half the time J.D. had driven it earlier, too anxious to get there to worry about a speeding ticket.

* * *

Zoe turned off the highway and started up the ranch drive with a small avalanche of magazines in the trunk. Sick at heart, still embarrassed by the store clerks' reactions to her bizarre purchases, she was light-headed with dread. From the looks of the magazine racks, not many copies had sold to anyone else, but once the clerks started gossiping about the goofy blonde who'd come in and bought every issue, everyone in the area would make an effort to discover what all the fuss was about.

No one in town but the doctor, his staff, the pharmacist and the diner waitress had seen her before. If she kept her car hidden away in the garage for a few days and stayed at the ranch, perhaps no one else would connect her with Hayes for a while—at least long enough for Jess to get home. After she made her confession to him, it wouldn't matter. By that time, the whole world would know she was on Hayes.

Zoe drove carefully into her space in the big garage and shut off the engine. Anxious to get a closer look at the magazines, she popped the trunk release and got out. She sorted quickly through the piles, trying to select one of every issue. She ended up with six. Too impatient to wait, she left the trunk open and leaned against the car to scan the covers and flip to the articles.

Tears of shame and frustration stung her eyes. The national rags were the worst, their headlines hyping scandal, the pictures dreadful, and clearly chosen to depict the Sedgewicks as villains. The only positive thing about them, she realized grimly, were that the pictures of her must have been selected to cast her in a better light.

Zoe's eyes were so blurred, she actually had to run a finger back and forth down the lines of print as she searched for the words Everdine, Hayes Ranch or Texas.

When she didn't find them, she went through each one again, not quite ready to believe she'd been that lucky.

She was scanning for names a third time when she noted that one of the scandal magazines was promising a four-part series of excerpts from the biography. That they would devote space in the next issue to excerpts which would detail Spenser/Zoe's life made her feel ill. If any article promised to reveal information about the children or the Hayes Ranch, that would be the one.

Zoe couldn't keep back the ragged sob that jerked up from her chest. She squeezed her eyes closed and gripped the magazine, unable to keep from giving in to several moments of misery.

J.D. watched silently from where he stood outside the open garage door. The brokenness he'd glimpsed in Zoe before was so starkly evident on her delicate face now, that he actually felt his chest hurt. It stunned him to catch her in an unguarded moment of such emotional distress. Because he sensed how deeply she'd be shamed if he walked in on her like this, he quietly backed out of sight, then took several steps away to give her privacy and time to collect herself.

J.D. had already figured she was Jess Everdine's daughter. She'd put herself in a hell of a spot with Jess, coming here the way she had. He hadn't dreamed that she was in any other kind of trouble, but seeing her crying over a handful of gossip magazines was evidence of that.

He knew he'd never get a straight answer out of her. Maybe Hollywood types learned early to be slippery, particularly when anything they said or did might be fodder for a gossip column. Zoe Yahzoo was as slippery as they came with that good fairy facade. Hell, the woman had everything but the wings and the magic wand that went with the image. J.D. couldn't imagine leading that kind of life, but something inside him understood, even if he didn't approve.

Uncertain how much longer he should wait, he called out a blustery, "Zoe Yahzoo, where are you?" in a ham-handed rhyme he figured she might normally appreciate.

Several heartbeats of time pulsed by before she called back a shaky-sounding, "A poet and he don't know it—" punctuated by the sound of the trunk lid closing. She stepped to the doorway, pushed the button to lower the door, looked his way and added, "But we can tell 'cause his feet are Longfellows."

J.D. chuckled at her corny attempt at lightheartedness, but he felt a new twinge when he saw how much effort she'd put in it.

"What are you doing, haring off to town? You're supposed to be doctoring wasp stings," he reminded her. Zoe started his way. Because he knew she wouldn't answer the question, he moved straight on with, "Carmelita said you weren't eating any cold leftovers from her kitchen. Got some of everything warming for you. Threatened to whack me with a wood spoon if I ate more than my share."

Zoe's smile was a little less forced as she scolded, "Now, J.D., I'm starting to suspect that you're deliberately trying to cast Carmelita as a skillet-bashing, spoon-whacking maniac. How could you malign such a sweet woman? You ought to be ashamed."

"Oh, darlin'," he said as he placed a big hand over his heart and turned to walk with her, "You have no idea the misery that woman has visited upon me over the years."

Zoe's much more normal "Get outta town," as she gave him a light jab with her elbow, gave J.D. an odd kind of thrill to have helped her regain some of her play-fulness. But as he glanced her way, the trace of pain still visible in her eyes made him feel guilty for encouraging her masquerade.

His expression must have sobered, because Zoe's abruptly did so, too, and those remarkable neon eyes shot away from his like a ricocheted bullet. J.D. angled his next step, bringing him close enough to take her hand and settle it companionably in the crook of his arm.

"Ever confide in anybody?"

Zoe's heart jumped at the blunt question. She stiffened, and would have pulled her hand away, but J.D.'s free hand pressed firmly over it to keep it in place. The choking emotions that overwhelmed her made her unable to speak. Oh God, had he seen her blubbering over those magazines?

J.D. drawled on as if she'd answered him. "I'm not much for hanging my private things on the front porch, either." They walked on a few more steps, the leisurely pace he set heightening her suspense. His big Texas drawl went so low that it was almost a whisper. "But then, I never had a partner before."

J.D., once he'd landed his little bombshell on her tattered emotions, said nothing more. Zoe couldn't have come up with an evasive response to what he'd said if she'd had a week to do it. Not when he'd just delivered the most profoundly moving offer anyone had ever made her. An offer to confide. Made by a down-to-earth man too honorable to tell another soul.

At that moment Zoe realized she loved John Dalton Hayes more than she'd ever loved anyone, more than she could imagine loving anyone else.

It was at that same moment that she realized how wide the chasm between them stretched.

*   *   *

Zoe didn't have much of an appetite for supper, but she did her best. She'd had a rocky few moments when she learned that Coley had sent some homemade ice cream. Because he'd thought she might not feel well enough to come down to the cook house, he'd sent up a generous portion. Zoe managed to make it to her room before she broke down.

Everyone on the Hayes Ranch had been good to her. They liked *her*, not because they were impressed with the Sedgewicks, not because she was rich, and not just because she was J.D.'s partner. Coley and Carmelita rarely bothered to pamper J.D., but they did her, and that only increased her guilt.

She was about to turn their lives upside down. Just the fact that Spenser Trevyn Sedgewick had been born and Zoe Yahzoo made selfish plans to indulge herself had put everyone on Hayes at ground zero.

And it would all be so much worse for Bobby and Becky. They were both wonderful kids, great kids. Sweet, innocent, and so refreshingly normal Zoe could hardly believe they were blood relation to her. But the book's revelations would traumatize them, tarnish their memory of their mother, and bring them the kind of notoriety and shame they'd never have been exposed to if not for Zoe.

If there was ever a time in her life when she wondered what earthly good Zoe Yahzoo's existence served, it was now.

About two o'clock that next afternoon, a pickup horn sounded from the ranch drive. The anxiety that had made Zoe half sick all day rose to such acute proportions she was certain her heart would beat out of her chest. She didn't need to hear Bobby's excited, "Dad's back!" to know who'd sounded the horn.

Bobby and Becky had come up to the house earlier that afternoon to use the pool, and had coaxed Zoe out to watch them swim. Now they toweled off madly and pulled on T-shirts and cutoffs over their swimsuits before they ran out to meet their father.

Zoe eased herself off the lounge chair she'd placed in the shade, but her knees were shaking so much it took her a moment to stand. She wished she was dressed in something more conservative than her cutoffs and a blouse with its tails tied up. Being barefoot didn't lend her any more confidence, but then, Zoe already knew she was a coward.

So much so that she nearly fainted when she heard the pickup engine rev. She listened to the sound of it turning in the wide drive to move toward the house near the highway. Being granted a bit more time before she approached Jess felt like a stay of execution to Zoe.

At the same time the reminder that she still had to face him made her anxious to get it over with. Zoe went into the house, then upstairs to sit a good long time in her room as she worked up the courage to do just that.

Much later, she heard Bobby and Becky return to the pool. J.D. had been gone to town on business for hours now, and Carmelita was in her kitchen working at preparations for supper. Jess might still be at his house, alone. With everyone nearby occupied and well out of earshot, there would be no better time to talk to him.

Zoe changed into regular work clothes. The stings were fading well enough to wear jeans comfortably, but Zoe wasn't focused on comfort. Time had run out for her— for them all—and she had to speak to Jess. She slipped out the front door quietly, then elected to walk down to the Everdines. Her hope that a brisk walk in the heat of late afternoon would take the edge off her anxiety was a futile one. By the time she stepped onto the side porch of the house and dared to knock on the door, her knees were rubbery with fear.

She scrunched her eyes closed, breathed a desperate prayer, then tried with everything she had to present something close to Zoe Yahzoo normalcy. She opened her eyes in time for the inside door to swing wide. Suddenly she was looking up into Jess's stern expression.

Zoe knew instantly his attitude toward her had changed. Which startled her because nothing she'd read in the magazines or seen on the news connected Bobby and Becky with her yet. She sensed the baffling anger that simmered beneath his cool countenance and felt her heart drop. Somehow, she found her voice.

"I was wondering if you had some time, Mr. Everdine?" Her throat spasmed closed when his expression turned stony. "I'd like to speak with you, if I may?"

The few moments that passed felt like an eternity. She offered him a hopeful smile, felt her mouth tremble at the corners, then let the smile fade as Jess's icy gaze bore down into hers. When he finally spoke, his voice had a hardness to it that wounded her.

"Haven't got time."

The drawled words were heavy with meaning, and a dozen tormented questions ran through her mind. She clutched desperately at a soft Zoe smile and tried again.

"It's really very important that we talk, Mr. Everdine. When would be a better time?" Zoe put great effort into stretching her smile wider, then felt it freeze on her lips when impatience passed bluntly over his handsome features.

"Look, Zoe, or Spenser—whoever you feel like being today. A better time came and went about five years ago." The twist of lips he gave her was bitter and harsh. "You said everything then that there was to say, and you were damned final about it."

Zoe's brittle smile vanished. Her bewildered, "What did you say?" was ruthlessly overridden.

"Just because some stray whim took your fancy doesn't mean that anyone else takes the same notion. I'd appreciate it if you went back to California and found yourself another little hobby. In the meantime, keep your distance from my kids." The warning in his voice drove through her like a lance. Somehow, she found the courage to try again.

"Please, Mr. Everdine. It's because of Becky and Bobby that—"

The violent slam of the door made her jump as if she'd been shot. Shock left her staring stupidly at the door, the rest of what she'd meant to say stunned from her lips as if she'd been slapped.

Reflexively, she raised her hand and knocked a second time on the frame of the screen door. The complete silence from inside the house was daunting, but she pulled open the screen and pounded urgently on the inside door. She had to speak to Jess, had to warn him. His bitter attitude toward her—whatever his astonishing statements meant—couldn't put her off. Bobby and Becky had to be prepared, they had to be protected. Zoe would suffer anything from Jess to accomplish that.

When the door remained stubbornly closed, desperation sent a frightening hysteria over her. "Mr. Everdine?"

His utter refusal to open the door to her resonated eerily with the most damaging experiences of her life.

Zoe sagged against the door frame, almost too weak to stand. My God.

The words were as much prayer as her wild thoughts could put together. In a fog of shock, she straightened and took a faltering step backward. The screen door closed with a soft thud that seemed to heighten the screaming whirlwind of pain in her chest.

My God. Zoe took another backward step. The tiny sliver of intuition that had quivered to life sometime during those traumatic moments when she'd stared up at Jess and heard his bitter words, now thrummed with certainty in her heart.

Jess Everdine was her natural father.

As Zoe turned dizzily and nearly stumbled down the porch steps, she saw that it all made horrifyingly perfect sense.

Look, Zoe, or Spenser—whoever you feel like being today ... The words tore across every insecurity she had, condemning her, calling down shame on who she had been, shaming who she was now. A pronouncement of deficiency that struck at the core of her muddled identity and declared her forever unworthy.

As the Sedgewicks had. Though Jason and Angela were far more subtle about it, it made perfect sense to Zoe that Jess would agree. Perfect sense.

Zoe's blurred gaze sought and rivetted on J.D.'s big house as she walked toward it in a mental and emotional daze.

Ever confide in anybody? J.D.'s low drawl came back to her so clearly she thought for a moment he was walking beside her. *I'm not much for hanging my private things on the front porch, either... but then, I never had a partner before...*

If Zoe hadn't been walking up the ranch drive where anyone could see her, she might have bent double with the pain those gentle words suddenly caused her. There'd been such a wealth of tenderness in them, such a bounty of meaning for someone who found it difficult to confide.

It didn't surprise her to realize that the pain J.D.'s words caused her now was because she knew they promised the impossible. For all the potential trust and real friendship they hinted at, in the end, they would prove to be no more than an emotional mirage.

Spenser Sedgewick and Zoe Yahzoo had chased enough emotional mirages. There were no truly loving and secure places for either of them. No place called home, no people to love who returned that love unless some mysterious standard was met.

The Hayes Ranch was no different. By the time she told J.D. about her sneaky manipulations and warned him about the trouble she was about to cause everyone—particularly the pain and shame her existence would cause Bobby and Becky—she'd be lucky if he didn't grab her and throw her bodily off Hayes ground.

Zoe finally made it to the house, letting herself in the front door as quietly as she could before she made her way to J.D.'s office, closed the door and picked up the telephone.

J.D. turned his pickup off the highway onto the graveled ranch drive, taking the curve too fast to keep the truck from fishtailing briefly. Something had happened. The growing certainty that it was something terrible stole the last of his pleasure at being granted the opportunity to get Hayes back.

The call from Zoe's lawyer in California had come through like magic just as he was finishing up late business with his lawyer. An offer to sell. Which he'd snapped up immediately. The paperwork had already been started before the idea started to bother him. Hayes would soon be all his. Every acre, every oil well, every head of cattle. His heritage, his pride. The moment he and Zoe signed the final papers and the money transfer was made, he'd have everything back that was rightfully his.

But why now? The question nagged him. Zoe had been on Hayes only eight days. Clearly, she loved the ranch and, unless he'd read everything wrong, the Everdines were her birth family. Which made this sudden offer to sell so shocking.

In the end, J.D. had called a halt to the process. His directive to his lawyer to put it all on hold until he could talk to Zoe had made the man red-faced with ire.

"Hell, J.D., a few days ago you'd have killed to get that one-third back. If the woman is this impulsive, how can you be sure she won't decide to back out—or sell it to those crazy environmentalists who were raising money to buy into Hayes before."

The part about the environmentalists had distracted J.D. He'd found out then that Zoe hadn't been the only buyer interested in Hayes. Raylene had managed to get more than market value out of Zoe for that one-third interest because Zoe'd had to outbid a radical group of grasslands preservationists. J.D. had been shocked to his back teeth over that bit of information. A fight with that bunch could have cost him a fortune and likely consigned a third of Hayes to public domain. Zoe hadn't breathed a word to him.

Which was all the more reason not to take advantage of her offer before he could find out why she was suddenly so hot to sell.

J.D. brought the pickup to a sliding halt next to the house and bounded out. He was late for supper, but the receptionist had called Carmelita for him. He wasn't surprised when he walked into the kitchen and saw the table set for two, but with no one in sight. A quick check of the top oven told him the food had been left warming so Carmelita could go along to some wing-ding at her cousin's for the evening.

It was then that the utter silence of the big house fully registered. Was Zoe even here? The heaviness in his chest dragged lower as he again got the sense that something had happened.

That feeling only escalated as he called out a loud, "Anybody home?" and got no answer.

CHAPTER SEVEN

ZOE heard J.D.'s pickup roar in and poured herself another three fingers of Jim Beam. She was sitting in one of the wing chairs in his office with the drapes drawn against the evening sun as she nursed a glass of whiskey. The pain had driven her nearly wild after she'd come back from Jess's. Calling her lawyer to arrange the immediate sale of her third of Hayes to J.D. had helped.

She ran a trembling finger around the rim of the tumbler and smiled grimly. Selling Hayes back to J.D. was a shameless bribe. A coward's attempt to make him feel too beholden to her to get nasty. Zoe raised the glass and took another bracing swallow of the amber liquid, noting that it no longer burned and choked her. Some of the sick knot in her middle had unraveled. Enough so that she muzzily considered that the vices of adult beverages might be vastly exaggerated. She'd never used drugs or alcohol in her life, never taken anything to blunt her pain or to help her screw up her courage.

But Jim Beam was proving to be such a dandy medicinal for both afflictions that Zoe decided perhaps the time had come to forsake such strict teetotaling. Take a break now and then. Feel better. No doubt Dillon Casey's book forecast at least one trip to the Betty Ford Center for pitiful little Spenser/Zoe. The offspring of the rich and famous seemed to migrate there in droves anyway. Why should she be so superior?

J.D.'s loud "Anybody home?" gave her only a mild start. The medicinal effects of Mr. Beam were making more of an impression by the moment, so Zoe gave herself a dose that finished off what was left in the tumbler. Then, with a doggedness she normally would have been appalled at, she reached for the nearby bottle.

She'd just poured and settled back when she heard J.D.'s booted tread in the hall. The smile of greeting she had for him when he stepped into the den was effortless.

"How come you've got the drapes drawn?" J.D. asked gruffly, then crossed to his desk and switched on the lamp. Zoe squinted against the soft light, then swung her gaze higher when he turned toward her.

"You gettin' snookered on my whiskey, Hollywood?" His short, surprised chuckle sounded more amused to Zoe than it was.

"Yep, John Dalton, I believe I am." She tried to focus on his face. "Did you get my message?" She grinned as if she'd made a joke, delighted when J.D. smiled back and slowly came her way.

"Seems like you're sending me more than one message, darlin'. What's going on?" J.D. dragged the other wing chair over and placed it in front of Zoe's before he sat down.

Zoe frowned. More than one message? The people in Texas talked in too many riddles. Jess Everdine was apparently a master at it. Even under the influence of Jim Beam, she still couldn't make sense of what he'd said. Now J.D. was doing it.

She leaned forward a bit to assert, "My *message*, J.D. Only one." She thrust herself back in the chair and had another sip as she waited for his answer.

"You mean about selling me your interest in Hayes? Yeah, I got that message, Zoe. I'm much obliged."

Zoe frowned. From the grim look on his face, J.D. looked anything but "much obliged." She tried a little smile. "It's a bribe, you know."

J.D. leaned forward and rested his forearms on his thighs. The smile he gave her deepened those wonderful creases on both sides of his mouth and curved them to his cheekbones. Zoe responded to the friendliness of that smile and leaned forward herself, resting her forearms on her knees, taking care to keep the stout tumbler balanced with both hands.

"What kind of bribe?" J.D. was still smiling at her.

Zoe's light brows crinkled. "How did you know it was a bribe?" she asked, then caught herself. "Ooops, I just told you, didn't I?"

J.D. nodded and gave another chuckle, but even quite mellowed out, Zoe saw the serious intensity in his dark eyes. His drawl was so low and slow when he spoke that Zoe thought it might be the sexiest voice she'd ever heard. "That was an awfully big bribe, honey."

He reached the few inches that separated them to wrap his hand gently around hers. That his long fingers also curved under the tumbler to give it extra support wasn't noticed by her. "What is it you're bribing me for?"

The soft question managed to find the well of pain not entirely numbed by the whiskey. Zoe didn't realize her grin went out like a bright light suddenly switched off. She was briefly too overcome with emotion to speak.

She finally got out a slightly slurred, "I've brought trouble to Hayes, John Dalton. Big, big, *big* trouble." It was a bit easier then to confess, "I won't be able to stand it if you hate me for it."

J.D.'s other hand came out to wrap around hers, his smile so tender and appealing that Zoe felt it reach into her heart and cradle it with the same warmth that his hands cradled hers.

"Well, now, Zoe, I can't imagine any trouble bad enough to make me hate you."

Zoe nodded emphatically. "Yeah, you could. About the time you find out what I've done and a zillion photographers and reporters show up to hound everybody." She was watching his face as closely as she could, but her little bombshell didn't appear to take away a speck of tenderness or appeal from it. Maybe he didn't understand. She tried harder. "Especially Bobby and Becky." An unexpected sob silenced her for a moment.

For several more, she fell prey to the number of things she'd meant to confess to him. They were whirling around in her head, mocking her attempt to organize them.

J.D.'s low, "What about Bobby and Becky?" seemed to help her focus. He covertly slipped the tumbler from her shaking fingers, then wrapped his big hands around hers and gripped tightly. The hard warmth and firmness of all those thick calluses was comforting. The tenderness in his dark eyes as he gazed over at her was wonderfully reassuring. She hoped it wasn't another mirage.

"Bobby and Becky's mother, Sarah, was my birth mother." Once she got that out, her thoughts seemed to get in a bit more order. "I don't know if Jess Everdine is my natural father or not, but I know he is." The contradiction escaped her.

J.D. gave her a gentle smile. "I figured that out, baby. The day you and Becky started the fence."

Zoe stared at him a moment, then released a sigh. "I knew it." She nodded. "But a big writer is doing a book on the Sedgewicks. He found out about Bobby and Becky and where they are. I couldn't get him to leave their names out—''

Zoe was overcome, resenting that Mr. Beam appeared to be letting her down. She got out a choked, "The reporters will be after them. They'll find out that our mother had an affair and that she gave up the baby. It will hurt their memory of her." Zoe bit her lips ruthlessly as she tried to hold back tears. "They'll be ashamed because of me. H-how will they get through it, John Dalton? What about their friends and the kids at school?"

She clutched his big hands urgently, her eyes searching his face as if to find an answer. J.D.'s grim expression registered, and the tender, easily hurt side of her nature quailed with distress.

"Now you understand why I had to bribe you." With that, she tried to pull her hands from his and stand, but he refused to release her.

"Whoa, there—sit still. Have you told Jess about this yet?"

Zoe's gaze fled his, too ashamed to tell him about her encounter with Jess that afternoon. She couldn't tell J.D., couldn't tell anyone she'd got what she'd deserved from Jess for sneaking into his childrens' lives. She hadn't been able to figure out most of the things he'd said to her, but the fact that he wanted nothing to do with her had been brutally easy to understand. Particularly his warning to keep her distance from his kids.

Look, Zoe or Spenser—whoever you feel like being today. She hadn't been able to down enough Jim Beam to numb the devastation those words had caused. It was certain she'd never repeat them to anyone.

"Zoe?" J.D.'s brusque tone demanded an answer. Her soft "No" made him give a grim sigh. "Then you've got to tell him. Tonight, if we can get you sober enough."

Zoe's alarmed gaze shot up to his, the haze of alcohol lifting to fill her mind with horror. She shook her head. "No—I can't."

J.D. was stern. "He's got to know, Zoe. You've got to tell him."

"I can't, John Dalton." Zoe shook her head emphatically.

His dark brow furrowed. "That's what you came here for, wasn't it? To find your family and warn them?"

Her, "Not entirely," slipped out. It took her a moment to realize her mistake.

"What do you mean, not entirely?"

J.D. was more persistent than she could handle at the moment. Zoe realized she was either too drunk or not drunk enough to evade him. His dark eyes probed relentlessly into hers and it struck her that she had to tell him the truth or he'd know that she hadn't.

But the truth was humiliating. And selfish, self-serving and pitiful. This really was the end, she thought dismally. If she told him the whole truth about why she'd come here as she had, it would be the last flaw. Hysterical giggles burst up and filled her eyes with tears.

"If I tell you, it will be the last flaw," she said, then paused because she'd said it aloud. "You've heard of the straw that broke the camel's back? Well, this will be the flaw that broke the—the—the what?"

J.D. shook his head. "Now you're making no sense at all, Hollywood. Think."

"I'm making perfect sense," she declared, sobering a bit. "I made perfect sense to me—my whole plan made perfect sense."

"What plan?"

"My plan to come here and see if Bobby and Becky could like me before they know who I am." Zoe hesitated when the impatience smoothed from J.D.'s face and she realized how excruciatingly intense his attention was suddenly. His expression was neutral, but Zoe interpreted it as the calm before the storm. The rest of her confession babbled out with unvarnished candor.

"I didn't want them to know who I was. I wanted to see if they could like me for me, not because of the Sedgewicks or because they felt they had to 'cause I'm their sister. I was going to win them over. I thought I had plenty of time before the book was released. I wanted them to like me before things got crazy. I didn't want them to know me the way Dillon Casey will tell about me. I—"

It was as much the increasingly grim look on J.D.'s face as it was hearing herself repeat the "I" word so many times that silenced Zoe. And made her feel ashamed to her soul. God, what a shallow, self-centered twit she was!

J.D.'s silence seemed to confirm everything she believed about herself. His somber expression was some sort of pronouncement on her. It felt just as shattering as Jess's, just as devastating as the Sedgewicks'.

Zoe gave him a wry, humorless smile as she thought how unanimous the consensus about her was. She didn't need to wait to find out what Bobby and Becky and everyone else on Hayes would decide about her. Some decisions didn't require much deliberation.

J.D. was still looking over at her, his expression as unreadable to her as hieroglyphics. But Zoe was suddenly weary of trying to read anyone, tired of looking for what she ached to see.

The drugging fatigue that suddenly swept her made the room spin and her body feel like it weighed a thousand pounds. Her eyelids were impossible to keep open, and she felt consciousness slip from her grasp as smoothly as a kite string.

J.D. caught Zoe easily as she slumped forward. She didn't so much as twitch as he shifted her to pick her up and stood slowly to his feet. Zoe was dead to the world, oblivious to everything, including the soft snores that might have made him smile at another time.

He'd known she was packing a load of secrets, but he thought he'd figured out most of them. He'd sensed the pain and brokenness behind her good fairy facade, but he realized now he'd glimpsed only a shadow of it.

Something had happened to her today. Something she hadn't admitted. There'd been nothing in what she'd told him that she couldn't have already known. She'd known about the book and that she had to warn Jess. She'd known her twisted-up reasons for coming here as she had, and she'd apparently already speculated about the book's effect on the kids.

For her to suddenly want to sell out then get rip-roaring drunk was some sort of reaction. Her sudden refusal to talk to Jess and warn him didn't make sense once she'd admitted that one of her reasons for coming to Hayes had been to do just that.

Unless she'd already tried. The more he considered it, the more the idea made sense. If she'd tried to talk to Jess and things had gone wrong, it could account for her raid on his whiskey and her refusal to talk to Jess now.

J.D. carried Zoe into her room and paused at the side of her bed. He might have let her sleep in her clothes, if not for the healing wasp stings. Because of those, he had to flirt with the torture of undressing her. He laid her gently on one side of the bed and methodically stripped off her clothes down to her underwear as he chivalrously tried to ignore her small, perfect body. He yanked down the bedspread and sheet on the other side of the bed, then lifted her over and tugged the covers up to her chin.

J.D. stared down into her sleep-soft features for a long time, thinking about what she'd said, more certain by the moment that his golden good fairy had got her wings crushed.

If she'd come here as she had because she'd wanted to see if Bobby and Becky would like her for herself, it had been a useless exercise. Everyone liked Zoe Yahzoo, everyone fell in love with her sparkle and fun. How could she not know that? What kind of upbringing did you have to have to even think up such bizarre shenanigans? Why had she thought she had to bribe him not to hate her?

J.D. grappled with the elemental difference between them, stunned that they seemed more starkly opposite than ever. It was this clearer sense of how vast their differences were that made him realize what a wild mismatch he and Zoe would make if either of them ever took Carmelita's marriage advice seriously. He didn't want to dwell on the reason for the unhappiness that suddenly blossomed in his chest.

He was turning to leave the room when his boot caught on the corner of a stack of magazines that peeped out from beneath the bed. He leaned down to push them out of harm's way, then caught sight of the inset photo near the corner of the top one.

It was a picture of Zoe, and she was dressed in a daringly cut black gown that fit like it had been painted on. Curiosity made him drag it out.

As he sorted through the stack, he saw that almost every cover featured some picture of Zoe with the Sedgewicks. That the headline article in each one was about the unauthorized biography sent a surprising flash of anger through him.

So this was what had brought Zoe to Hayes. J.D. scanned one or two of the articles as he crouched there by the bed, but was too disgusted to glance through them all. The outrageous invasion of privacy and the tawdry sensationalism of the articles made him furious. As he shoved the magazines back under the bed and straightened, he couldn't help but look over at Zoe.

Deeply asleep, her soft cheeks flushed and her short wedge of platinum curls sparkling on the pillow, she looked too vulnerable and fragile and pure to be the subject for the cheap tripe of scandal sheets.

The astonishing idea that she was anyway jarred him.

Zoe awoke sometime near ten that next morning. Her head was pounding, and the foul taste in her mouth made her nauseous. It took several moments for her to figure out why she felt so awful. It took no time at all for her to pronounce a heartfelt curse on Jim Beam and his ilk. She carefully rolled to her side and slid off the bed, teetering as she tried to get upright and stay that way.

It dawned on her as she navigated from the bed to the bathroom and the shower, that she'd neglected to remove her underwear and put on her pajamas the night before. The reason she'd somehow foregone her normal routine escaped her. Which gave her faint alarm. She hadn't realized before now how much she relied on her wits to deal with the world. The fact that her mind felt dull and slow gave her the disturbing sense that she was off kilter and vulnerable.

The sharp needles of hot spray peppered through her hair to her scalp as she washed her hair and showered. She waited until the hot water ran lukewarm, then stepped out and grabbed a towel. She managed to dress and take dreary note of the time before memory kicked in. When it did, the resulting plunge of her heart made her wish she'd stayed in bed.

"The *señor* told me to tell you it has hair of the dog that bit you."

Carmelita plunked a tall glass before her as she sat in her chair at the breakfast table. Zoe stared suspiciously at the chilled concoction that bore shades of color from yellow to deep orange to red. As she picked it up and gave the liquid a testing swirl, she noted sickly that some of it clotted together with the consistency of lumpy slime. Her stomach pitched and she quickly set it down.

"It is the *señor*'s family remedy for hangovers."

At the stern thread in Carmelita's tone, Zoe glanced up, then felt her face warm. "What's in it?"

Carmelita's dark brows winged up in an arch. "You could drink half a bottle of whiskey, but are worried about this?" She gave a wry chuckle and waved her hand. "Drink it all. And remember with regret what you did that made you have to drink this."

Carmelita's clear disapproval was softened by the sparkle of humor in her dark eyes. That the woman was amused at Zoe's self-inflicted predicament—and the glass of what was plainly as much punishment as cure—stirred Zoe's sense of humor and lifted her dismal spirits. Carmelita still liked her. For now.

Zoe stared at the horrid concoction, then gamely picked it up under Carmelita's watchful eye. At her last-second hesitation, the woman crossed her arms over her chest and gave her a stern look to prompt her. Zoe scrunched her eyes closed and forced the contents of the glass down, having no problem at all remembering with regret why she had to drink the awful mixture that bore the thick taste of raw egg, cayenne and tabasco. That it also carried the strong taste of whiskey must have been what Carmelita had meant by "hair of the dog that bit you."

Zoe thumped the glass down with a gusty sigh of relief. Carmelita whisked it away, returning in a moment with a small stack of dry toast and a bottle of aspirin.

Her stomach went into near-public revolt. Zoe was halfway off her chair for a mad dash to the bathroom before the wave of nausea magically calmed. She eased back down, beginning to feel better. By the time she downed some aspirin, finished the toast and dared a cup of coffee, Zoe felt almost human.

But without the physical misery of a hangover to distract her, the events of the day and night before began a ghastly parade through her thoughts.

Had she really failed so utterly with Jess and made such a fool of herself with J.D.? She remembered most of what she'd confessed to J.D., but she remembered every expression on his stern face with aching clarity. Particularly his terrible grimness once he'd known the extent of her self-centered folly.

She agonized over that and almost reached a private vow to never face J.D. again when she heard a boot-step on the porch. The back door swung wide and he walked in.

"Hungover?" His big voice boomed good-naturedly as his dark eyes homed in on hers.

Zoe's gaze fled his. She couldn't bear to see how disgusted he must be with her. The fear that he might also make her face Jess and subject herself to further agony was stronger still.

She wasn't surprised at all when J.D. told her, "Jess is coming to the house. You can have that talk with him."

Zoe sprang to her feet and shook her head. "I can't now, J.D. You know what he has to be told so he can prepare the kids."

"You want me to tell him?"

The question made her send him a grateful look. "Yes, please. And a million thanks for doing it."

J.D. shook his head, his expression more grim and purposeful than she'd ever seen. Anxiety gave her a painful jolt. "I'm not going to do it for you, Hollywood. You've got to face this."

Her small, "I can't," made no impression.

"Do you love those kids?" The blunt question was a reproach.

Zoe nodded faintly. Her weak, "You know I do," was choked.

"Then you've got to do it." The stern statement thrust at her.

Zoe couldn't look away from the dark solemn eyes that silently warned he would be disappointed in her if she didn't. It struck her then that J.D.'s good character wouldn't have allowed him a moment's thought or hesitation if there was some moral right he felt he had to do. Cowardice or the threat of emotional devastation wouldn't give him even a second's pause.

But it gave Zoe hours of pause. She was a coward to the core and she didn't have enough good character to push through a buttonhole. Coming here in the sneaky way she had to play her foolish little like-me-for-me game was irrefutable proof. J.D. didn't seem to understand that his expectations of her were lofty, and about as difficult for her to meet as height requirements for a model.

And yet, as she looked over into his implacable expression, Zoe realized she valued this man's approval too much not to try. She loved J.D. precisely because he was the man he was and, though the coward in her was screaming in protest, she also loved that he was leaning heavily on her to do the right thing. She'd needed someone her whole life to set a moral parameter, someone to rein in her natural exuberance and set a fair, clearly defined standard for her to live up to.

J.D.'s hard work and good character measuring stick was fair, down-to-earth, and eminently practical. Zoe realized with some surprise that she'd do almost anything to meet it. Whether she ever had a chance to win J.D.'s love or not, and even if the Everdines never accepted her as kin, she'd never be able to live with herself after this if she didn't make the effort.

"I'll do it." The words didn't come out very strongly, but then, Zoe didn't consider that she should waste what little strength and resolve she had on any definitive statements to J.D. Not when she needed it all to face Jess again.

Once she'd agreed, it took almost no time at all for J.D. to bustle her to his office. It was astonishing how quickly Jess showed up, but it wasn't surprising at all to see that he appeared less than thrilled to be present in the same room as her. Because she'd not known the best way to begin, she'd dashed upstairs moments before Jess's arrival and grabbed her stash of magazines.

When J.D. abruptly exited the room and closed the door behind him, Zoe almost lost her nerve.

The two times she dared to glance Jess's way, she noted his expression was as hard as a brick, and that he wasn't looking her way at all.

Nervously, she crossed to him and held the stack of magazines out. "A popular author who specializes in scandalous, tell-all, unauthorized biographies of celebrities is doing a book on my adoptive parents." For a dizzying few moments, she thought Jess wouldn't take the magazines.

"I saw your picture on some of those in Ft. Worth. That's how I found out who you really are." Jess's brusque tone was little more than an accusation and Zoe's heart fell.

He finally took the magazines. She passed him the last one separately and called his attention to the line that promised the next issue would print a detailed excerpt from the book on Zoe's life with the Sedgewicks.

"That's the one I'm worried about. I hired investigators to find S-Sarah, but none of them ever came up with anything. When I realized Jason and Angela had regularly gone behind my back to buy them off so they would conveniently fail, I hired someone out of state. He found Sarah, but—" Zoe couldn't bring herself to say the words "but she'd died." "But he found out that she had two other children who lived here."

Jess's restless shift in the wing chair made her foreshorten most of the other details about buying into Hayes and coming here to get to know the kids before she disclosed who she was. Zoe acknowledged that she was still too cowardly to confess everything to Jess. She rushed on before he became too impatient and cut her off.

"Someone who worked for the investigator heard about the author's latest writing project and sold him the information about Bobby and Becky."

That at last earned her Jess's full attention, but the harsh gleam in his eyes was livid with accusation.

"I-I went to the author—Dillon Casey is his name—and tried to get him to leave Bobby's and Becky's names out of his book and not to reveal their location on Hayes. But the hallmark of his books are the details. He has no fear of lawsuits, since he considers them nothing more than pricey publicity."

Zoe paused for a horrifying moment because of the killing intensity in Jess's eyes. "So I failed to persuade him to leave the kids' names and location out of print. The huge popularity of Jason and Angela and the widespread public attention toward anything or anyone connected with them will—"

Jess's furious swear word, and his near launch from the wing chair, made Zoe spring back.

"So what you're telling me is, my kids are gonna be hounded by the press and have their mamma and daddy's private history laid out in public."

Zoe found a shred of courage as he leaned aggressively toward her. "T-that's what I'm telling you. And that it's my fault."

Her soft words seemed to take a fraction of the aggression from his belligerent stance. But her equally soft, "I'm so sorry," seemed to rile him all over again.

His eyes blazed down into hers. Zoe imagined she saw the blue fire waver a moment and go out. But the moment was so quick, she must have imagined it, because the next second it rekindled and forced her gaze to flee his.

His low, "Stay away from my kids," seared her soul.
She almost fainted when he charged from the room and
let the door swing wide. Through blurred eyes, she gazed
stupidly at the stack of magazines that had somehow
scattered to the floor. Numb, she bent and picked them
up. She hefted the lot into the small garbage can next
to J.D.'s big desk before she quietly exited the room.

CHAPTER EIGHT

ZOE hadn't been able to find the courage to face J.D. She hadn't been able to even look at Carmelita on her way out the back door. She felt restless and wild inside, and more than a little betrayed by the disheartening reward of doing the right thing—however belatedly.

She ended up at the garage, and went through the side door to where her car was parked. The bright red color glowed even in the shade and Zoe opened the door to get behind the wheel. She reached for the garage door opener on the dash, aimed it, then listened to the sound of the big door motoring up. She slipped the key into the ignition when the door reached the end of the track and thumped to a stop.

Moments later she backed out and turned around, rocketing down the graveled drive to leave an enormous rooster tail of Texas dust in her wake. She slowed to turn onto the highway, then hit the accelerator again.

The hot wind that buffeted the car and raked through her bright curls seemed to blow her miserable thoughts away to a safe distance. The hard pressure of her small foot on the accelerator pushed the car to the limits she'd guessed at, but heretofore had had too much sense to explore.

But the sun was bright, the sky was blue, and the strip of Texas highway before her was as empty as she felt. The mirages she chased on the pavement drew her inexorably forward.

Just like all the other mirages, she reflected bitterly.

* * *

It was hours before Zoe's wide, whirlwind tour of Texas highways put her on the highway back to town and the Hayes Ranch beyond. The state trouper who'd clocked her doing a hundred and ten through his speed trap in another county had threatened to arrest her on the spot, but he'd caved quickly to Zoe Yahzoo charm.

She hadn't been able to charm him out of a traffic ticket with a godawful fine, however, but her close encounter with Texas law enforcement had instantly converted her into a law-abiding citizen. She'd driven no more than the speed limit after that and felt her wild emotions calm in proportion to the discipline of adherence.

She'd driven through town and was almost halfway to Hayes when she saw a car off to the side of a rise ahead. She automatically slowed when she saw that the driver already had the car on a jack. Her heart gave a painful twinge when she recognized the car and the young blonde who stepped out from behind.

Becky Everdine had caught sight of her red convertible, because she was suddenly waving her arms to get Zoe to pull over. Leery of disregarding Jess's demand for her to stay away from his kids, Zoe slowed her car, turned it around, then pulled up behind the Everdines' car. Becky bounded over to her before she could get out.

"I gotta flat, Zoe. I got the tire off, but the spare is flat, too. Can you give me a ride into town to fix it?"

Zoe had instant misgivings, but a quick glance in the rearview mirror showed the highway to Hayes was as empty as the highway into town. The midafternoon sun was hot along the pavement. There was no way she could refuse to give Becky a ride.

She made herself grin up at Becky, glad for the sunglasses that would conceal the effort. "Toss the tire in the trunk. We might as well get air in the spare while we're at it," she said, then popped the trunk release and got out to help. Once both tires were in the trunk and they were strapped into their seat belts, Zoe checked the mirrors and pulled out.

"Thanks, Zoe. I was afraid I'd have to walk."

Zoe's, "No problem," was light but, she hoped, not an invitation for more conversation. She didn't want to know if Jess had told the kids anything yet, and she certainly didn't want to know what he'd told them.

She'd already decided during her long drive to pack her things and move to a motel in town until the papers for the sale of Hayes were ready to be signed. She needed to break as swiftly and cleanly from Hayes as possible since she knew Jess would want her gone.

Her family was unattainable. She didn't think she could stand to know for sure that J.D. was, too. It helped her dismal expectations of the future to believe J.D. would always be here on Hayes, and that perhaps there was a sliver of something wonderful possible at some future time too distant to calculate.

The whole idea gave her another mirage to chase, but she reckoned she'd survived too much of her life on mirages to break the habit.

They reached town a few minutes later, and Zoe slowed the car. She turned into the full-service gas station and pulled off to the side. She popped the trunk release and Becky got out to get one of the attendants. Zoe took off her sunglasses and got out, too. She waited until the attendant got the tires from the trunk to take them into the service area before she called Becky over to the soft drink machines.

"How about a soda?" Zoe invited. "My treat." They made their selections, then took them over to a bench in the shade of the station.

"Can I ask you something, Zoe?"

Becky's hesitant tone sent a charge of dread across Zoe's nerve endings. She hoped her pretended distraction as she glanced down the street and her vague-sounding "What?" would discourage Becky from asking anything too serious. She'd felt Becky's close scrutiny more than once on their short trip to town. She'd sensed then what was coming, known it with queasy certainty. When Becky fidgeted tensely beside her, Zoe braced herself.

"Are you really my...sister?"

The words landed on Zoe's battered heart like a knock-out punch. She glanced down, gave her soda can a swirl that stirred the contents, then had a quick sip.

"Are you, Zoe?"

Becky's soft prompting pushed at her. Zoe lowered the can, then gave in. She glanced over into Becky's earnest expression.

"Yes." Zoe looked away, then leaned back on the bench with a sigh. "I'm selling out to J.D." She gave a shrug. "I was on my way back to pack my things when I picked you up. I'll be leaving as soon as the papers that sell back my percentage of Hayes are ready to sign."

Becky touched her arm. "But you can't leave now. Bobby and I want to get to know you."

Zoe shook her head to that. "Not now, honey. Maybe when the two of you are older—" She swiftly amended it to, "Definitely then," and gave Becky a small smile.

Becky's face crumpled a bit. "Daddy will get over being mad," she said urgently. "I told him you must be sorry about what you wrote in that letter, or you wouldn't have come all the way here."

Zoe's attention fixed instantly on the mention of a letter. "What letter?"

"The letter you wrote Mama and Daddy." Becky frowned.

Zoe turned more fully toward her and reached over to grip her hand. "What letter?"

"You know about the letter," Becky chided. "You wrote it."

Something twisted sickly in Zoe and she shook her head. "I never wrote a letter. I *should* have before I came here, but I didn't." Zoe didn't realize the frown of confusion on her face so closely mirrored her sister's. "What do you know about a letter?"

Becky was looking at her strangely, but she complied. It was quickly evident to Zoe that Becky was still young enough that the details babbled out with a youthful lack of tact.

"Mama and Daddy hired an investigator to find you after you turned eighteen. He found out you were adopted by movie stars, who you were, and where you were. Mama and Daddy wrote you a letter—Daddy says he thinks they might have rewritten it a dozen times so they wouldn't sound like hicks from Texas to you, since you lived in Beverly Hills and all that."

Zoe's breathing went ragged as she listened to what Becky was saying. Jess and Sarah had sent her a letter? Had that been what Jess was talking about yesterday when he'd told her that a better time to talk to him had come and gone five years ago?

It hurt to hear Becky's little aside—that she'd seen their mother make a tiny, barely visible mark on the kitchen calendar for every day that passed between the day they'd mailed their letter, and the day Sarah found a letter from California in the mailbox. It had arrived four weeks to the day, typewritten on elegant paper in a chic, lined envelope.

But the gist of the message was that Ms. Spenser Trevyn Sedgewick, who felt a ranch foreman's family had nothing to offer her, wouldn't much appreciate being bothered by further contact from the Everdines. *You said everything then that there was to say, and you were damned final about it,* Jess had said.

Zoe lifted a trembling hand to her head, heartsick at the stark cruelty of the letter—the letter she'd never, ever, have written. The horrible suspicion that flashed to life made her head spin as Becky chattered on.

"Mama refused to throw the letter away. It's still in her keepsake box. She made all kinds of excuses to Daddy for you—Spenser is young, her life is probably filled with so many glamorous, exciting things, we'll give her time to mature..."

Becky's voice trailed off abruptly. Zoe was alert to the idea that Becky had just realized how distressing this all was for Zoe and that she suddenly regretted giving so much detail. Zoe lowered her hand and looked over somberly at the upset on her sister's face. Her instincts told her there was a bit more to the story.

"What else?"

That there was something more was evident by the tremor of Becky's lips and the way her worried gaze flinched from Zoe's. Zoe gripped her hand. "Please. Tell me the rest, Becky."

Becky shook her head and Zoe tried again. "I swear to you, honey, if I had ever gotten a letter from them, I would have come to them right away. I looked for our mother—" Zoe broke off, reluctant to confess the details of the pitiful search she'd made during her childhood. "Let's just say I always, *always* tried to find her."

"Then who sent the letter?"

The answer to Becky's question roused the rage and frustration Zoe had felt for as long as she could remember. Rage at the Sedgewicks' power to control and manipulate the life of a child they barely cared for, frustration that they still practiced their manipulations at more levels than she was aware of, despite her efforts to thwart them. Nevertheless, to actually tell her young sister who she suspected of writing the cruel letter was difficult.

"Probably Angela." The words were low, but she looked over into her sister's face and persisted softly, "Tell me the rest."

Becky bit her lip in indecision and Zoe hazarded her most painful guess. "They never got over the letter, did they? Especially Sarah."

Becky's eyes filled with tears and several shot down her cheeks. "She wouldn't throw the letter away. Sometimes, she'd have nightmares and I'd hear her crying. She'd tell Daddy she'd dreamed you were hurt somehow or that you needed her, but she could never do anything to help you. Then Daddy'd get upset and tell her that she'd done the best she'd known how to do at the time and that giving you up was *his* fault, not hers."

Zoe couldn't bear another word and sprang to her feet to gulp in air as she drove her fingers through her bright curls in agony. The whirlwind of rage and pain and heartache was so profound that she suddenly felt faint.

"Oh, Zoe—sit down—please!" Becky was at her side, trying to take her arm.

Zoe shook her head and moved shakily toward the outside entrance of the small women's rest room. Becky let her go and Zoe shut herself in.

The terrible knowledge that Sarah Everdine's emotional suffering over her lost child had been so acute made what Zoe had suffered in her growing up years suddenly seem so much less important. Whatever pain and loss Zoe had weathered, at least it hadn't been compounded by the crushing guilt Sarah had clearly borne for giving her up. That theirs had been a companion pain which could have found solace five years before while Sarah was still alive left Zoe breathless with anguish.

But their one precious opportunity to find each other had been stolen away. The all-important letter so carefully written by Sarah and Jess because they feared they might sound like hicks from Texas to their materially privileged child had fallen into merciless hands. Cruel hands that had penned a reply which had caused Sarah agony for the rest of her life.

It was no wonder Jess had been so harsh with her, she realized dizzily.

Zoe bent her head, her slim body shaking as the knowledge of the bitter tragedy impacted her more deeply. She was too shocked to cry, the pain was so profound. She didn't know how long she stood there with her arms wrapped tightly around herself before the worst of the tremors passed and her stunned emotions struggled sluggishly to adjust. At last, she stepped forward to the small sink and shakily twisted on the cold water tap. Mindful now of how long Becky had been kept waiting, she dashed her hot face with water and dried off with a wad of paper towels. She made a last effort to collect herself.

The knowledge that nothing could ever undo this terrible wrong for Sarah left her desolate inside. As she stepped outside and rejoined her teary-eyed sister, Zoe wished with all her heart there was.

Desperate to function, Zoe offered her sister as much of a normal smile as she could. "Do you suppose those tires are ready?"

Becky nodded. "They just put them in your trunk. Are you all right?"

Zoe reached out and wrapped an arm around her sister's shoulders to walk with her to the car. Her soft, "Please don't worry about me," was choked, and she tried to smile.

"Do you think your father would believe me if I tried to tell him that I didn't write that letter? Without any proof other than my word?"

Even if she could somehow convince Jess, she wasn't certain it would make anyone but her feel better. And even that would be marginal now. Still, she didn't want Angela's cruelty to continue to be credited to her.

Becky frowned anxiously. "I don't know. I'll tell him I believe you."

Zoe shook her head. "No, honey. Please don't intervene for me. I don't want to come between the two of you." She couldn't bear to be the cause of a rift between her sister and father. From all she'd seen so far, Jess had a loving relationship with both kids, and she didn't want to hurt that.

They reached the car and Zoe dropped her arm as they parted to go to their separate sides to get in. Becky suddenly caught her hand.

"Would you stay, Zoe? Please? At least for a few days?"

"I don't know," she answered softly. "It's probably better to go."

"No—that can't be better," Becky urged. "Maybe J.D. could talk to him for you."

Zoe's heart was dealt fresh pain at the mention of J.D. Leaving Hayes and her family was a reminder that she was also leaving him. The instinctive knowledge that J.D. was one of a kind, and somehow the only man she could ever feature loving and wanting to be with for the rest of her life made the future seem unbearably bleak.

"No," she said quietly. "I don't want to put J.D. in the middle, either."

"But, Zoe, you can't just—"

The loud blare of a horn and the roar of a pickup engine as it swung off the street and barreled into the service station lot startled them both. The pickup tires squalled as Jess hit the brakes and slid to a stop beside Zoe's convertible. He was out of the truck in an instant, his face flushed with anger. He was shouting before he'd gone two steps.

"Becky—get in the truck."

Zoe's low, "Hurry, Becky," and the panicked look she sent her made Becky rush to comply with her father's order. Becky's quick compliance didn't deter Jess, who came around to the back of Zoe's car and towered over her.

"When I told you to stay away from my kids, what the hell did you think I meant?"

Zoe couldn't look away from the tight anger on his face. Oh, God, this was her father. He was crushing her, destroying her hope and making it impossible to imagine there was any way to get through to him. Her gaze faltered, and she leaned briefly toward her trunk to key it open and lift the trunk lid.

She looked up into her father's face. "I know what you meant, Mr. Everdine. You'll need to get Becky's tires out of my trunk."

Jess couldn't seem to stop glaring down at her those next ominous moments. In those moments, what Becky had told her about Sarah's nightmares came back to Zoe on a thread of intuition that blazed like lightning.

Daddy'd get upset and tell her that she'd done the best she'd known how to do at the time, and that giving you up was his fault, not hers. His fault, not hers. The words speared into the fresh wound of his relentless rejection. The idea that this man had somehow initiated the chain of events that had devastated Sarah's life and her own, yet was laying the blame on Zoe, made it impossible not to strike back.

The wild pain in Zoe surged up. She gave him a bitter smile as the tormented self-doubts and insecurities of a lifetime spewed forth.

"So, how did it happen, Mr. Everdine? Did you take one look at me and tell Sarah, 'Nope. Let's not keep this one'? Was my arrival not convenient for you, or did you get a good look at me and see some terrible flaw that didn't make me worth keeping?"

Jess's hard face flushed and the harsh intensity in his eyes was livid with pain. The knowledge that she'd dealt him a bit of the crushing pain in her own heart was not nearly as satisfying as she'd hoped.

Not even her equally bitter "It appears you were something of a prophet," as she turned from him and stalked to her car door, gave her a glimmer of the satisfaction she'd grabbed for.

The moment she felt the weight of the tires lifted from her trunk, she started the engine. The sound of the lid slammed shut set off her roiling emotions like a starter pistol. She shoved her foot down on the accelerator and shot out of the service station lot, the volatile emotions she could barely control speeding her toward Hayes.

The overwhelming need to be with J.D., to hear his gruff drawl and somehow try to soak up a bit more of his granite steadiness came over her in a wave that made her hurt. She suddenly craved the feel of his big arms crushing her against his hard body. She was starved for another taste of him, for one rough male kiss that would imprint him forever on her heart and mind. Somehow, she had to have that from him—something from him— something she could carry with her when she left Hayes.

She had to leave Hayes. Tonight. She considered she was, after all, just as gutless and shallow as ever, because she'd reached the limit of what she could take from Jess. The knowledge that he was tough and virtually heartless would make him an absolute nightmare for any reporter who might try to hound Bobby and Becky. No one in the area would ever dare give the kids grief about their parents' youthful indiscretion. Because of their formidable father, the Everdine children would weather whatever was ahead with ease.

There was no reason for her to stay. Her continued presence would either drive a wedge between the kids and their only parent, or compel them to side with their father and spoil any chance Zoe might have for a relationship with them when they were grown.

Though the prospect of a future relationship with Bobby and Becky was probably just another mirage, for Zoe, it was just about the only thing she could see in the distance.

CHAPTER NINE

"You have been gone such a long time!" Carmelita exclaimed as Zoe let herself in the back door. When Carmelita came her way with a look of care and concern on her sweet face, Zoe almost broke down. "We were worried."

Zoe's crooked smile was the best she could do. "My apologies, *señora*. I didn't mean to worry you." She shakily reached out to the Mexican woman and touched her arm. "I hope you won't be offended if I don't have some of that wonderful supper I smell. I'm not hungry tonight. I'm going . . . upstairs."

She couldn't seem to put together the words that would tell Carmelita she meant to pack her things and clear out. Not when Carmelita's soft brown eyes were searching her pale features for the details of the upset she'd sensed—and genuinely seemed concerned about.

It was a relief when Carmelita allowed her a quick escape. Once she reached her room, she crossed to a small closet where she'd stashed her boxes and luggage. She dragged out one of the larger pieces and opened it on the bed, then turned to start with the clothing in her dresser drawer.

The sound of J.D.'s heavy tread coming down the hall made her glance toward her open door just as he came into sight.

His imposing height filled the doorway. "You worried hell out of me, Hollywood." He came her way and Zoe flinched from his stern expression.

She struggled mightily to reclaim the lighthearted personality that played off J.D.'s prickly gruffness like magic. She needed something of J.D., some last something special, some last opportunity to experience what made him profoundly irresistible to her.

She looked at him and tried a Zoe Yahzoo smile that fell as abysmally flat as her desperate intentions.

"Does that mean you like me, John Dalton?"

"It means you worried hell out of me," he repeated gruffly.

Zoe's smile widened to cover the fresh jab of pain to her chaotic emotions. "Oh, that's right," she said lightly. "I haven't signed the papers yet, have I?" She gave his arm a pat and crossed the last steps to her dresser to yank open a drawer. "Don't worry, J.D. Before I came to Texas, I added a few lines to my will that ensure my interest in Hayes will return to you immediately in the event of my death or diminished capacity."

She gasped when J.D. grabbed her arm and swung her toward him. "That's a hell of a thing to say."

Zoe rallied. "It's a hell of a fact, John Dalton. Who I know, what I own, and the size of my bank balance is everyone else's prime concern. Why wouldn't it be yours, particularly since Hayes is your birthright?"

J.D.'s expression was thunderous. All at once, Zoe felt ashamed for the insult she'd dealt him and her gaze fled his. She made a slight move to free her arm, then turned away and covered her burning face with her hands.

"Oh, I'm sorry, John Dalton." Her whispered words caught on a hitch of delayed reaction. She dropped her hands and wrapped her arms tightly around herself. "You didn't deserve that." The sob of despair that jerked out made her bite her lip to hold back the others. Her soft, "Is there any way you can forgive me?" was barely audible.

She was badly startled by the warm, hard fingers that closed over her narrow shoulders and gripped gently. She squeezed her eyes closed, both to contain the hot tears that were blinding her, and to focus on the wonderful comfort of his strong, sure hands.

"I'd like us to part friends," she whispered, hating the faint hint of desperation in her soft voice.

J.D.'s voice was equally soft, but with the gravelly texture Zoe loved. "Why? Are you going somewhere, Hollywood?"

Zoe couldn't suppress the violent shaking that quaked through her as she summoned as light a tone as she could manage. "Yeah, I think I've pretty much worn out my welcome in this part of Texas."

The violent shaking became more pronounced as J.D. stepped close and his big arms came around her from behind to lash her firmly against him. "Who says?"

Zoe gave a shrug. "Oh, I can pretty much tell." Of their own volition, Zoe's fingers sought the hard-muscled definition of J.D.'s thick forearms and closed over them greedily.

His hard jaw settled against her cheek. "Jess gave you a hard time?"

"No more than I deserve," she said quietly, then took a wavering breath. "You should have heard the appalling things I said to him. I had no idea I'd picked up any of Angela's capacity for bitchiness." She turned her face toward his. "I didn't mean to inflict any of that on you, John Dalton, honest. I really do... admire you, you know." A brief smile touched her lips. "I wish I was half the man you are."

J.D. groaned at that. "If you were, we'd make a hell of a picture standing here like this." He turned her in his arms, his dark eyes serious as he looked down into her pale face. His big hand came up and lifted her chin when she tried to evade his close scrutiny.

"I don't give a damn what kind of tangle you and Jess got into, aside from the fact that you're hurting over it. I don't give a damn who thinks you've worn out your welcome at Hayes. You're my partner, Zoe Yahzoo, and as long as you are, you need to stay on Hayes and live up to your one third of the partnership."

Zoe's heart was squeezing madly with tenderness and gratitude for J.D.'s gruff words. How she loved this big man. She gave him a crooked smile, unaware of the sad little bend to it as she reminded him, "But we're about to sign papers and you're going to transfer a whopping fortune into my bank account that will dissolve that partnership, John Dalton."

J.D.'s stern features relaxed the tiniest bit. "Hell, Hollywood, you know lawyers and how they like to gum up the works haggling over which i's to dot and how many t's to cross. No telling how long it'll take 'em to come up with something we can sign."

Zoe did get teary then. "Why are you doing this?"

"Maybe I'm trying to return the favor."

His statement made no sense to Zoe and she blinked hard to get a clearer look up into his dark eyes. "What favor?"

J.D. reached up and tugged gently on a bright curl. "That little favor you did me by outbidding those environmentalists."

Zoe's gaze fled his self-consciously. "When did you find out about that?"

"Yesterday." His hand caught her chin and redirected her gaze back to his. "So I owe you a big one, Zoe."

She shook her head emphatically. "You don't owe me a thing. I bought into Hayes for my own selfish reasons, not because I meant to do anything particularly noble," she said hastily. "Please don't credit me with any golden character traits, John Dalton. I don't have very many."

J.D. glared down at her, but the glimmer of tenderness in his dark eyes softened it. "I'll do whatever I damned well please, since I own the majority of this partnership—how about something to eat? I'm hungry as hell."

His quick change of subject caught her by surprise. She shook her head, about to tell him she wasn't very hungry, when he suddenly started her toward the door.

"You'll feel better once we get a hot meal in you. Carmelita's gone off to her sister's for the evening, so you can tell me all about what's going on between you and Jess."

Zoe allowed him to usher her along with his big hand firmly on the back of her waist, until they were partway down the stairs and she had second thoughts. She glanced J.D.'s way.

"I'm not so sure you should know any details, J.D. I don't want to involve you in any more than I already have."

"Too late for that, darlin'. I'm in up to my tan line," he declared as he kept her moving down the stairs. The surprising fact that he didn't appear at all annoyed confused her.

She let him shepherd her to the kitchen and sat down without protest when he pulled her chair out for her. It touched her that he gamely picked up a pair of pot-holders and got their supper out of the oven. She stared down at her plate as he sat the platter and bowls on the table, tossed down the pot holders, then took his usual place across from her.

His gruff, "Better get something on that plate and eat up," was so bossy it made her smile. She reluctantly complied, cut into her steak and had a first bite. The rich flavor stirred her appetite and before long she'd managed to get down a full supper.

It amazed her a little when, after they finished eating, rinsed their dishes and loaded them in the dishwasher, J.D. didn't press her to talk. Instead, he escorted her down to the cook house for a bowl of Coley's ice cream and her usual cut-throat game of checkers with the cook. It was dark by the time they walked back to the house.

Zoe felt better after their meal and a bit of her normal routine at the cook house. Her emotions didn't feel nearly as volatile, but she was suddenly weary beyond belief.

All of that changed the moment they stepped into the ranch kitchen. On their way out, J.D. had switched off every light but the one on the range hood, so the mood of the big house was quiet and soothing. The coward in Zoe hoped she could get by with simply crossing the kitchen to the hall door and make a casual escape upstairs to bed. But J.D. caught her arm the moment he'd closed the porch door.

Having recovered a bit of her Zoe sparkle, she let him turn her toward him and gave him a smile. The determined line of his mouth was clear, even in the soft light.

"Uh-oh, John Dalton. Why do I suddenly think you're about to do an impression of an old time Texas Ranger who would ride into hell—or at least as far as Mexico—to get his man?"

The line between J.D.'s dark brows deepened. "Why do I suddenly think you're about to throw sand in my eyes and make a run for the border?" he answered softly.

His big hand came up and he settled his hard palm against her cheek. Zoe couldn't keep herself from reaching up to press it tighter to her pale skin. The compulsion to turn her head and place a kiss on his callused palm was too strong to resist. Her lashes drifted closed as she did. After a moment she slid her lips away and rubbed her cheek against his palm. The patience she sensed in him made her dare a look up into his dark eyes.

"How big is that front porch you mentioned the other night?" she asked softly, but the off-hand smile she tried wobbled a little.

J.D.'s deep voice was a gravelly rasp. "As big as it needs to be, darlin'."

Zoe put up a hand to stifle a sound that was part chuckle, part sob. J.D. turned her toward the doorway to the hall and wrapped his arm around her shoulders. They walked to the darkened living room and sat down together on the sofa.

Before she knew it, the details of her encounters with Jess flowed out, along with a pained repeat of what Becky had told her about the letter and its tragic impact. When she finished, she was so appalled by the wracking sobs she could no longer keep back, that she abruptly pulled away from J.D. She leaned forward with her elbows propped on her knees and her hands pressed over her face in a vain attempt to muffle her anguish.

J.D. leaned forward himself and placed a hand on her shoulder to give it a bracing squeeze. She tried desperately to recover.

"S-sorry. I'll stop in a moment. I don't have a habit of doing this, you know." The spasm of sobs that followed thwarted her intentions. J.D.'s hand slid off her shoulder and Zoe suddenly found herself across his lap, facing him, cradled tightly in his arms. Her arms went around his neck.

Despite her effort not to, she finally gave in to the deluge of tears. It didn't help her control at all that J.D. whispered gruff encouragement to her to let it out as he kept her firmly on his lap. The worst of the tears passed, but still J.D. held her, his big hand moving up and down her back in a slow, soothing motion. He took his hand away only long enough to shift them both and dig a handkerchief from his back pocket.

Zoe took it gratefully, then hurriedly unfolded it and put it to enough use to reduce it to a damp ball. She subsided against him, her cheek snuggled against his wide shoulder.

J.D. let out a slow breath. "This is going to come out all right, Zoe." His big hand smoothed gently over her curls.

Zoe didn't agree. But the hallmark of Zoe Yahzoo had always been her ability to appear unfazed by the things that would give normal mortals pain. Coming to Texas had thrown her performance off badly, but it was time to reclaim the image. Zoe leaned back a bit and grinned tiredly at J.D.

"You aren't one of those annoying optimists, are you, John Dalton?"

"I don't need to be an optimist. All it takes is knowing the people involved. Jess Everdine would no more let his own flesh and blood go down the road never to be heard from again than I would. He'll come around."

J.D.'s opinion gave her heart a sharp pang. She had difficulty maintaining her smile. "That's probably true with Bobby and Becky."

"It'll be true with you, too, Zoe."

Zoe shook her head and looked away as her smile faded. "Please don't say that, John Dalton." She felt J.D.'s solemn scrutiny. His voice was thoughtful and low.

"You don't understand much about what blood relation means to some people, do you?"

She didn't need to think about her answer. "I know what it means to me. I always believed it might have made a difference with Jason and Angela if I had been their natural child." She shrugged. "I know what it will mean to me when I have children—if I do." Zoe stopped there. "If" had more to do with J.D. than she wanted him to guess.

J.D.'s voice was just as thoughtful and low as it had been, but it was somehow softer and quieter. "What will it mean to you, Zoe?"

The emotion that overwhelmed her at his unexpected question made it difficult to speak. The surprising fact that she wanted to answer helped, and she looked at him in the dimness. "It will mean that there's nothing I wouldn't do for that child." Her gaze shifted away and she tried to moderate the fierceness of her declaration. "I had a lot of years to make vows about how I would raise a child, how I would make him or her, or—even better—them, feel secure and loved and wanted. I'd be careful not to spoil them too much, I'd hope—"

Zoe cut herself off, suddenly self-conscious. Lord, what would she know about raising a child? Given the Sedgewicks' horrid example, her theories about raising children were based on what she'd fantasized about as a child, what she'd seen on the family-run ranches she'd lived on and what she'd read in books.

Her voice was quiet and a little choked as she subsided against his shoulder. "I can't talk about that anymore."

J.D.'s arms tightened. She took a quick breath and forced a lighter tone to change the subject. "Anyway, Bobby and Becky are great. They know about me now. I think someday—"

To her dismay, she couldn't put her hope for someday into words, either. It was a surprise to find she had a superstitious reluctance to jinx the possibilities by speaking them aloud. Besides, to her it sounded pitiable to declare any particular hope for the future where the kids were concerned after things had gone so terribly wrong with their father.

"I'm sorry. I don't mean to chatter on and on." She leaned away from J.D. to give him a small smile. "Like I said, I think I've worn out my welcome in this part of Texas. And, though I appreciate that you're trying to do me a favor by holding up the sale, I think it's best for everyone to get the papers signed right away.''

Zoe couldn't maintain eye contact with the intensity in J.D.'s gaze and looked away. She made a small move to signal she meant to get off his lap, but his arm tightened. He reached up to turn her face.

''Right now, I don't much care for what's best for everyone else, Hollywood,'' he said as he made her look at him.

In the next instant his lips seized hers, the pressure of his big hand on the back of her head forcing her mouth hard against his. Zoe's initial surprise vanished, and she was suddenly kissing him back with a wild enthusiasm that took no account of tenderness or propriety.

This was what she'd craved, a rough male kiss to dominate her senses. A kiss and a taste so compelling and hard-driving that it made mush of every thought and reduced her to a mass of nerve endings and sensations. Zoe gave herself wholeheartedly, soaking in every electric tingle, not wanting to miss even a heartbeat of the sensual delight she wanted to remember forever.

Sometime in those fevered moments, J.D. worked open more than half the buttons on her blouse. His bold fingers edged beneath the lace of her bra to her breast, toying with its sensitive peak delicately, but with devastating expertise. She was so overwhelmed with sensation that she gasped for breath and clutched at him.

Her breathless ''Make love to me, John Dalton,'' was little more than a mouthing of the words, but

J.D. heard. She was dismayed when his fingers began to ease away. Her quick move to place her hand over his to keep it where it was thwarted his retreat by only a quick scattering of seconds.

Then, despite her clear signal, J.D. slipped his hand from beneath hers. That his kiss became more urgent was an apology of sorts—a kind of consolation prize, Zoe reckoned dizzily as frustration stormed through her.

Her frustration was so acute as the kiss began to mellow that she found herself on the verge of begging for more. She managed not to shame herself by actually doing so. When he finally moved his lips from hers and crushed her tightly against him, Zoe battled the sting of tears as the sensual whirlwind began to ebb.

Zoe realized then that she wasn't the only one trembling with desire and disappointment. J.D.'s big body was practically quaking with it.

But the fact that her passionate request had spoiled everything sent Zoe's heart into an inevitable plunge. The worst thing she could imagine—asking for love and being denied—was once again terribly routine for her. Her emotional jinx appeared to have already seized the high ground in sexual matters, and Zoe felt a new kind of hopelessness.

Suddenly restless, possessed of the unbearable need to escape, Zoe straightened, her face flushed with shame and useless effort as J.D. stubbornly kept her where she was. She was grateful the room was too dim for him to see the extent of her upset as she put everything she had into speaking.

"Does this mean you've reconsidered?" she asked, striving for a light, flirting tone, relieved that she'd managed it.

"I'm not going to take advantage of you, Zoe." J.D.'s low words were calm and resolute.

Zoe leaned toward him in the dimness and planted a quick kiss on his mouth. "I'd take advantage of you in a minute, John Dalton," she joked, but her heart was aching. J.D. would have been the first man she'd ever allowed that close. Not that anyone would believe Zoe Yahzoo had never lost her virginity, not when Jason and Angela's sexual exploits were frequent and modern morality so lax. She'd been offering J.D. Hayes a lot, but he didn't want it. The idea that she couldn't get close enough to him for even a quick fling was another hard punch to her wounded heart.

"Well, since that hot little kiss has fizzled for you already, I'd like to get on up to bed. I've had a hell of a day, John Dalton. I could use a good night's sleep." She felt his hold relax and she slid off his lap, wavering a moment when she came to her feet before she got her bearings in the dim room. J.D.'s big hand caught hers, delaying her new attempt to escape.

"That hot little kiss is going to play hell with my good night's sleep, Hollywood," he grumbled. "Just because I'm not going to take advantage of you tonight when you're stirred up about your family, doesn't mean there won't come a time when I'll take everything you've got."

J.D.'s words were an iron-clad vow. That was Zoe's first impression. An instant later she took them as kind words from a man who, underneath his gruffness, was compassionate and generous.

And that made her feel pitiful and needy. Her light, "Another time then," carried a hint of melancholy she couldn't help. Zoe slowly pulled her hand from his and made her way around the sofa to the stairs. There'd never be another time and J.D. knew it. Zoe hated that she knew it, too.

Zoe tiredly prepared for bed and crawled beneath the covers, worn out, but unable to forget the very best of her time with J.D. that night.

For a tough, blunt Texan who spent his days working with dangerous, contrary animals in the brutal Texas heat, J.D. was an astonishingly gentle man. In spite of his sexual rejection of her, everything she'd sensed about him was somehow much deeper and wider and truer than she'd suspected.

How did you win a man like John Dalton? How did you make a place in the life of a man who was so secure in himself, so strong and self-sufficient? Zoe desperately took stock of the things she had to offer.

Money, property, celebrity connections, looks and an entertaining, never-met-a-stranger personality. The liabilities that came with the package included troubles with his foreman, the celebrity and notoriety of the Sedgewicks, Zoe's damaged upbringing and a history of eccentric pursuits that ran the gamut from wildly speculative stock investments to her role as a sought-after pseudo-star on the edges of the Sedgewicks' phenomenal success.

Hardly the traits a solid, down-to-earth man like John Dalton Hayes could tolerate in any woman for long.

Zoe had already come to the conclusion that she'd not actually lost anything she'd already had by coming

to Texas to find her family. She'd never had much of
a family with the Sedgewicks, she probably never
would with the Everdines. The fact that she had hope
for a future relationship with Bobby and Becky was
actually a plus on the gains side of her personal ledger,
something that should have made this whole traumatic trip to Texas worthwhile.

But J.D. had skewered her tally sheet of gains and
losses. He'd scrawled his name across the top of a
new sheet, his very existence altering her focus and
redirecting her emotional goals. Despite her dismal
assessment of the things she had to offer and her
chances of winning J.D., Zoe wasn't surprised to
realize that when the time came to put the final mark
in one of the columns beneath his name, she still
hoped with all her heart the mark would land in that
wide, pristine space beneath the gains side.

"How are you, Zoe?" J.D.'s gentle question as she
took her usual place across the breakfast table from
him that next morning gave her worn heart a soft lift.
The bright smile she gave him won a cautious half
smile from him that deepened the creases on one lean
cheek.

"Much better, thank you." Zoe glanced Carmelita's
way. "What's for breakfast, señora? I'm starved."

"That is good," Carmelita nodded approvingly.
"You will have steak and eggs and the shredded potatoes very brown as you like them, but I have also
made your favorite."

Zoe's light brows shot up with delight. "I was
hoping those were cinnamon rolls I smelled. I hope
you made lots."

The rest of breakfast went as Zoe intended. She beat J.D. to the comic section of the Sunday paper and read it aloud to him between bites as he tried to read through the business section. She thoroughly enjoyed the leisurely Sunday morning meal, as usual, chiding J.D. for his early morning grumpiness and trying a mild flirtation or two. Despite her crushing disappointments, particularly the one with him the night before, she meant to make the most of as many more mornings and days and nights as she had left on Hayes.

The last thing she wanted was to leave Hayes like a whipped dog with its tail between its legs. Pride dictated she leave with as much dignity as she could summon. When it came time to load her things in the car, she wanted to be every bit the playfully flamboyant, tin-foil-shallow Zoe Yahzoo who'd arrived that first day.

CHAPTER TEN

JESS Everdine had spent another hellish night. Sunday had dawned too early for him. He was in too black a mood for church, though he imagined Sarah would have gently chastened him with the reminder that spending the morning in the Lord's house could fix that. He'd sent the kids off to Sunday School without him, his conscience nettled by their somber faces. That they both were upset and disappointed in their daddy was no secret.

Neither of his children could resist championing Zoe. They'd managed to force everything they knew about her on him, chronicling every minute they'd spent with her as well as making it clear that they meant to keep in touch with her. His small family was in an uproar, but it was nothing compared to the uproar in his own heart.

So, how did it happen, Mr. Everdine? Did you take one look at me and tell Sarah, 'Nope. Let's not keep this one'? Was my arrival not convenient for you, or did you get a good look at me and see some terrible flaw that didn't make me worth keeping?

Zoe's bitter words haunted him. The pain he'd seen in her eyes was still vivid in his memory.

It appears you were something of a prophet. Those last words had hammered home the strong impression that for all Zoe's remarkable good looks and wealth, there was something wrong about the way she saw herself.

He regretted his words to her when she'd first tried to talk to him. *Look Zoe, or Spenser, whoever you feel like being today . . .* If Zoe was half as insecure about herself as he now feared, those words must have devastated her.

Jess knew he was a prideful, stubborn man. He hadn't realized his capacity for cruelty.

Sometime during his long, restless night, the letter Spenser Sedgewick had written five years ago had ceased to matter. She'd been given away at birth. If she'd thought her mama and daddy hadn't wanted her as an infant when she'd needed them most, then she'd probably resented that they'd suddenly decided to barge in on her rich Hollywood life when she was grown. Jess regretted that he hadn't understood that. He regretted being so harsh.

Jess bent his head and dug his finger and thumb into the corners of his eyes as he tried to contain the powerful emotions that churned in his gut.

Zoe Yahzoo was his child, his and Sarah's. The cockeyed way she'd tried to enter their lives no longer mattered, either. The fact that she'd finally tried made all the difference. It was past time to let her know.

Zoe's morning ride was soothing. Because the routine on Sunday was quite lax on Hayes compared to the rest of the week, she'd packed her saddlebags and gone off on Brute. This might be her last chance to have the run of Hayes and enjoy it, so she meant to make the most of the opportunity.

J.D. was in his office bringing his paperwork up to date, so to avoid making herself a total pest, Zoe had elected to go riding. She still meant to seize every minute with him she could, but later, after he was finished.

The day promised to be a hot one, so she rode Brute on a route that would parallel one of the creeks. By the time the sun got high enough to get really hot, she and Brute could return to the headquarters, making full use of the shade from the long line of cottonwoods along the creek bank.

Zoe needed the peaceful ride. She hoped it would restore her in some way, heal her from all the other needs that seemed doomed to be forever thwarted. She was already feeling better. Thinking about Sarah still pained her, but the knowledge that there was nothing she could do about her birth mother now dampened a bit of the restlessness in her. Sarah must have wanted her, even if she had given her up. Zoe might never know the exact reason, but the idea that Sarah had searched for her consoled her in some mysterious way. She didn't let herself think about Jess. There were still some things too distressing to think about.

She drew Brute to a halt on a ridge that overlooked the creek and gave her a panoramic view of the wide, empty range land that surrounded her. The wind was blowing hot, but strong enough to relieve the bright heat of the sun.

She'd finally looked her fill at the vast expanse before her, exhilarated by the mammoth size and distance, awed by its overwhelming size. She turned Brute toward the creek before she saw the rider who waited on the opposite bank below.

Zoe's father was a big man. He sat his horse easily, confidently, and she recognized him instantly. The impression Zoe got—that he had sought her out—gave her as much hope as terror. It was too late to pretend she didn't see him.

The impatient toss of Brute's head made her aware
that she'd pulled back on the reins. The bay must have
picked up her sudden tension, because he pranced rest-
lessly and worked at the bit as he waited for her to signal
her next command.

She couldn't move, and didn't know if she was dismayed or relieved when Jess made it for her. His lanky
buckskin stepped forward, walking sedately through the
creek as he crossed to Zoe's side. The buckskin continued up the gentle slope toward her, his unhurried pace
giving her emotions time to crank to full throttle. She
was certain she'd faint by the time Jess eased back on
the reins to halt his horse beside Brute.

"You weren't given up because there was anything
wrong with you, Zoe." Jess's low words were rough, but
the harshness she expected to see on his face was re-
markably absent. "The wrong was with your daddy and
mama. It's a story you need to hear. If you want."

Zoe stared at her father. There was a tenderness about
him that caught her off guard. She couldn't mistake the
weary pain in his eyes, or the tiny glint of hope and
anxiety she saw there.

She dug up a panicked dose of Zoe sparkle to mask
the dread that persisted. "Will this be a new version of
'Go away, kid, ya bother me'?" The quirky little smile
she gave to cover her distress trembled despite her best
effort.

The choked breath Jess took in startled her, but the
thick tears that deepened the blue of his eyes did not.
"No, baby." He reached over a bit awkwardly to touch
her hand. "Not again, not ever."

Zoe couldn't help that she turned her hand over and
gripped his. She was so overwhelmed she couldn't speak.

"Your daddy has a history of stupidity when it comes to recognizing the best things that come along in his life. The good Lord has always had to work a little overtime to bring me around to another chance." Jess appeared overcome for those next seconds before he could go on. "I'm hoping He's gonna give me that second chance one more time."

The tears that tumbled over Zoe's lashes to splash down her cheeks gave Jess the only answer she was capable of.

Jess Everdine and Sarah McCauley had been sweethearts since the seventh grade. Sarah dreamed of a wedding after high school graduation, a home and children. Jess had rodeo fever. He'd wanted the wedding, the home and the children, but later, after he'd won the money to finance the life he'd wanted to give Sarah. As the son of a poor rancher, he'd wanted more for Sarah than his father had been able to give his mother. He'd also wanted the thrill and cowboy glory that went with being a champion bronc rider.

By their senior year of high school, he'd competed locally and won enough times to show promise. The itinerant life-style that would enable him to travel and see the country greatly appealed to a boy who'd grown up with the hardscrabble drudgery of working a broken-down spread with a father who'd grown old and sick before his time. Plagued by hard luck, an unreliable water source and enough bad markets and poor health to break his spirit, Sam Everdine had encouraged Jess's rodeo ambitions.

Sarah had been born into a prosperous ranch family. She'd wanted Jess to work for her father. They could have the old homestead house, and when her parents passed on, he could work for her older brother. Jess's pride wouldn't allow him to marry into money and live as a hired hand to his rich inlaws.

They'd finally come to an outright argument the day after graduation. Sarah declared that she never wanted to see him again. He'd been happy to oblige her.

She'd change her mind when he won the buckle and the money, he'd reasoned. She'd be glad later when he could buy them a nice place of their own.

Jess didn't call her at all the first year he was away. When he finally did, it had been Independence Day more than a year later. But Sarah had been cool on the phone, sounding more distant than the eight hundred miles that had separated them. She didn't take his calls after that.

Meanwhile, he won the National Finals in bronc riding. He'd won the buckle and the prize money he'd wanted, but he'd given up on Sarah. And, his daddy had been dying. The cost of keeping the ranch going for his mother and paying for the experimental cancer treatments the insurance wouldn't cover ate away at his winnings. In the end, his father succumbed and their debt-ridden ranch had to be sold. The money they cleared from the sale and what was left of Jess's winnings went to buy his mother a nice house in town and provide her with a modest nest egg.

He'd returned to the rodeo circuit for another year, but never made it to the national finals again. He finally burned out on rodeo. He came back to Texas, but only as far as the next county north of where he'd grown up. He wasn't broke, but with only a few thousand dollars in the bank, he had nowhere near what he'd need to buy a place of his own.

He'd hired on as foreman on a midsize ranch. He'd worked there several months by the time he'd gone to a

Saturday night dance. To his surprise, Sarah McCauley had been there with some friends. Still unmarried and unable to completely ignore him, she'd given in to his request to dance. He promptly dominated her time on the dance floor.

Jess had thought of her nearly every day of the five years since their breakup, but had long ago given up on the idea of a second chance with her. But now she was at last in his arms, and the old feelings came back for them both. He'd not wanted to squander the unexpected opportunity to win her back. At least as a ranch foreman, he had something to offer. It was less than what he'd wanted to give her, but it would be a decent life, and they could raise a family.

To his dismay, his quick proposal was met with a sad little refusal from Sarah. That's when he'd learned about the baby she'd given up—his baby. She'd figured he'd never forgive her for not being able to withstand her family and that the news would make him change his mind about wanting to marry her.

Jess had been torn apart by the story, further humbled by the fact that he'd left Sarah pregnant and alone while he'd pursued his selfish dream of rodeo glory. Knowing their firstborn daughter was long gone, they'd married and had two more children. They'd saved money over the years so they'd be ready to hire a good private investigator to find her when she turned eighteen.

As Becky had told Zoe, once they found her and tried to make contact, the letter they'd received for their efforts had broken their hearts. Sarah had initially suffered a hard bout of depression. But, Jess was careful to emphasize to Zoe, the year before the car accident that had taken Sarah's life, her sunny disposition had reappeared. Her optimism about one day hearing from

Spenser when she had children of her own and experienced motherhood for herself had been as strong as her vastly restored good spirits. There'd been no more nightmares that last year of her life, no more tears. Sarah had found peace, and Jess had found a measure of peace himself.

Until he realized Spenser Sedgewick had come to Texas with a new name....

"John Dalton! Are you here?" Zoe's excited call as she entered the kitchen from the back porch went unanswered. "J.D.?"

She quickly hung up her hat and started for his office. The late afternoon silence of the big house didn't bother her at first. Carmelita spent most Sundays with her family, so she hadn't expected her to be around.

The profound happiness Zoe felt was about to burst out of her chest, but a bit of it ebbed when she reached the den and saw J.D. wasn't there. A hurried trip upstairs told her he wasn't in the house at all. Undaunted, she rushed back out through the kitchen and hurried to the long garage. J.D.'s pickup was gone.

Zoe went back to the house feeling a little deflated. J.D. had predicted that Jess wouldn't let her go down the road never to be heard from again. He'd been right and she was eager to tell him so. She stepped into the kitchen and closed the door, then sagged against it, delirious with happiness.

Jess had answered the questions she'd carried for a lifetime. Knowing how she'd been given up and why had made a deep impression on her. The ill-defined perceptions she'd held about herself her whole life had shifted somehow and refocused. She hadn't been flawed or unlovable; she'd not been given up because Sarah and Jess hadn't wanted her. For the first time in her life, she began to feel settled inside, rooted, real.

She'd been the product of young love that had lost its way, but never quite died. Jess and Sarah's story had been sad, tragic in parts, but underlain by the kind of enduring love and tenderness Zoe greatly envied.

And hoped to have with J.D.

Zoe felt a new rush of happiness and thrust herself from the door to cross the kitchen and head upstairs for a quick shower. Perhaps it was just as well that she'd have some time alone. Once she and Jess had talked things out and gone to his house for lunch, Bobby and Becky were back from church. Becky had been putting the finishing touches on the meal.

After their happy reunion, they'd eaten, then Jess brought out the family photo albums. Zoe's head was still spinning from the number of people she'd seen in the albums. Though Jess was an only child, his family of aunts, uncles and cousins was enormous. Zoe had no idea how she'd ever figure out who was who and how they were all related, but Jess promised she'd have a dandy chance to make a start when she attended the Everdine family reunion planned for early August.

Zoe Yahzoo was on top of the world.

J. D. Hayes had rarely experienced true misery. Even Raylene's dramatic exit from his life, their pitched court battle and the partial loss of Hayes in the divorce hadn't produced this boot-dragging, heart-heavy ache.

But now that Zoe's fun and sparkle had been centered almost exclusively at the Everdine's house these past three days, J.D. was feeling a letdown he'd never felt before. The lion's share of her time was now spent with her father, sister and brother. Jess's mother, Agnes, had come over from Keswick two days ago to meet her long-lost grandchild, further dominating Zoe's attention.

J.D. was happy for Zoe. The brief time they did spend together over breakfast and the few minutes they had when she came back to the house late in the evenings just before bed, had shown him clearly that what he'd sensed about Zoe before had changed.

Zoe was no longer so melancholy and broken inside. She seemed surer about herself somehow, less fragile. She still smiled her megawatt smiles, she still sparkled and she was the same fun, flirtatious Zoe he'd found so irresistible. But the sparkle and fun now went deeper than her carefully projected surface image. Zoe was truly becoming the smile-spangled, irrepressible imp she'd pretended to be, and J.D. was more powerfully taken with her than ever.

He didn't know what he'd do once the papers were signed and she finally went back to California. He wasn't sure he could stand knowing his future connection with her would be solely through the Everdines. Besides, Jess was interested in a small, successful ranch over in the next county that would come on the market by spring. If Jess bought it as he planned, J.D.'s hope of seeing Zoe when she came to visit her family would be much less certain.

J.D. had rarely experienced true misery, but the notion that Zoe had lost interest in him was one of the sharpest disappointments of his life. The knowledge that she would take a huge hunk of his heart with her when she packed up her sparkle and fun and left Texas, made him feel every bit the grim, humorless, *lonely* man he'd been before she'd shown up and waved her magic wand.

He had no idea how to reclaim her attention and see if he could tell whether all her past flirtations meant anything now. He wasn't sure he should even try.

Zoe received a package on Thursday. It had been lying on the table by the front door when she'd come in and she'd noticed that it was addressed to her. The weight and shape she felt through the padded mailer sent her high spirits down several notches as she inspected it for a return address.

Glad that Carmelita was in the kitchen preparing supper and hadn't heard her come in, Zoe hurried upstairs for privacy. She closed the door to her room and crossed to the bed, her knees suddenly shaky as she sat down on the edge of the mattress.

She'd all but forgotten the biography. The past few days had been the most wonderful of her life. Her only regret was that she'd not spent much time with J.D. and she missed him terribly. She'd come back before supper today to begin to remedy that, but the package delayed her plan.

Zoe's hands shook as she dug her short nails under the flap and pulled it open. She took a deep breath, slipped her fingers in to grip the edge of the hardcover book, then pulled it out. Zoe didn't let herself look at the book jacket until she checked to see if there was a letter in the mailer. When she didn't find one, or any other indication of what had sent it, she set the mailer aside.

The Sedgewicks Offstage: Behind the Lights and the Legend by Dillon Casey. The words flashed up from raised gold-foil lettering against a shiny-black book jacket.

She stared down at the dreaded tell-all book. Suddenly filled with the anxiety that had been so blessedly absent these past days, she forced herself to open it. Beginning with the first page, she began to scan for the words Becky, Bobby, Everdine, Hayes Ranch or Texas.

Somewhere in those first pages, the other words Dillon Casey had written began to penetrate. Gripped by a terrible combination of curiosity and mortification, Zoe went back to the first page, unable to keep from reading every word.

She never heard J.D. come in downstairs, was too absorbed to remember to let anyone know she was in the house or to go down to supper. As she worked off her boots and scooted up to sit on the bed with her pillows wedged between her back and the brass scrollwork of the headboard, she kept reading.

It was hours before she finished, hours before she was absolutely certain of everything Casey had put into print about Bobby and Becky. That he'd changed their names to Danny and Sherry Anderson was as shocking a surprise as the fact that he'd named the state they lived in as Montana instead of Texas.

The horrors she'd anticipated him writing about the Sedgewicks were worse than she'd imagined. That Casey had found out about the letter Jess and Sarah had written her and had printed a copy of the cruel response was another stunner. He'd named Angela as the one who'd written it and emphasized that her malicious interference had prevented Zoe from meeting her biological mother while she was still alive.

The fact that he'd guessed that Spenser's summers of migrating from one dude ranch to another had been a secret, desperate search to find her real mother caused Zoe the only real pang of embarrassment. He'd got nearly everything he'd disclosed about her upbringing and her relationship with her adoptive parents right. What astonished her was that he'd done so in such a way that would make the reader strongly sympathetic to Spenser/Zoe.

She felt a little better about it, particularly since he'd not made her sound too pitiful. And if changing the kids' names and location and giving her a fair portrayal in his book hadn't been enough, Dillon Casey had gone easy on any predictions of doom and gloom for her future.

Zoe realized her face was wet when she finally set the book aside. The unexpected pity she felt for Jason and Angela, however much they might deserve having the details of their lives so brutally exposed, kept her in her room until well past time to make it down to the cook house for ice cream.

She considered calling the Sedgewicks to express some sort of sympathy for the chaos and upset the book would cause them. She gave up the idea when she realized that anything she said to them now on the subject would provoke a bitter accusation of blame. A simple, vague note that said something along the lines of "I hope you are well and weathering it all with your usual aplomb" would be sufficient.

Zoe took a few moments to call Jess on the phone extension in her room. He was relieved that Casey had changed the kids names to throw off the media. She elected to wait to tell him that Casey had named Angela as the author of the cruel letter. Jess already believed she hadn't written it herself. The whole subject was now unimportant to him.

Besides, everything was going wonderfully for them all. *Almost* everything, Zoe amended as she glanced at the clock on her bedside table and realized how late it was. She wouldn't get much of a start on making up for lost time with J.D. tonight.

She did need to let him know she was in the house, however, and got up to do so. She'd opened her door to step into the hall when she heard him come up the stairs.

"Hey there, J.D.," she called to him. He glanced her way, his harsh expression softening.

"Hey there, yourself, Zoe. Things going well for you?" The tired half smile he gave her as he walked down the hall toward her did great things for the long cheek creases she liked so much.

Zoe gave him a smile. "Very well, J.D. How about you?"

"Good enough."

She suddenly wanted to touch him, to somehow banish the weariness she sensed about him. But J.D. reached up to tug gently on a bright curl beside her cheek and went on walking down the long hall.

Her soft, "Good night, John Dalton," was answered with a low, "'Night, Hollywood," before J.D. stepped into his room.

CHAPTER ELEVEN

"THE lawyers have the papers ready to sign," J.D. told her that next morning at breakfast. "Any time you're ready."

Zoe frowned at the information and finished chewing her bite of steak. His low, "If you still want to go through with it," made her hurry.

"I certainly do want to go through with it, John Dalton," she hastily assured him. "Hayes is your inheritance. It's not right that anyone but your children should have a piece of it. Let's sign today. You name the time."

That Zoe was still in an almighty hurry to sell was clear to J.D. He didn't want to examine too closely the disappointment he felt. Zoe gave him a sparkling look and one of her imp smiles.

"So, how many children do you plan to pass Hayes on to, John Dalton?"

He grunted and took a last bite of steak so he wouldn't have to answer that. Zoe chattered right on.

"I hope you don't do the usual and only consider leaving it for your firstborn son to run. You might have a daughter or two who'd do a dandy job of it."

J.D. grunted again, but Zoe barely hesitated.

"You should have at least one daughter who can ride and rope and run the place. Send all your kids to college for degrees in agriculture." She aimed her fork at him. "But make sure you raise them to keep as many of the old ways as possible. Stay traditional. No helicopters,

172

motorcycles or feedlots. Send at least one child to law school so there can be a potential state legislator, or maybe even a congressman or U.S. senator in the family to influence legislation that benefits ranching interests.''

She took a last bite of breakfast and watched J.D.'s grumpy expression darken.

"You've got my kids raised, planned their college, and mapped out their careers before five-thirty in the morning, Hollywood,'' he groused.

Zoe gave him a chiding smile. "You're what? Thirty-four?'' She shook her head and gave a wave of her fork. "You have a *lot*—'' she rounded her eyes for emphasis "—of time to make up for, John Dalton. You need to make some ambitious plans and dedicate yourself to getting a few of them going. Life's not all sweat and hard work.''

Zoe sprang up from her chair and flitted away from the table before he could recover. By then, she was at the sink filling her thermos and complimenting Carmelita on another breakfast "well done.'' Carmelita was tittering over what she'd heard of their exchange. Zoe turned back to him and slung her saddlebags over her shoulder. Her light brows crinkled as she took obvious note of the fact that he still sat at the table.

"I thought you were done eating, J.D. Come on, shake a leg. Vacation's over for the summer.'' With that, she was at the door, had her hat on and was reaching for the doorknob. She practically vanished, leaving J.D. halfway out of his chair, a heartfelt snarl of frustration rising from his chest.

That Carmelita stood at the sink grinning at him, gave J.D. the distinct feeling that he was the butt of some female joke he couldn't begin to get.

He got his hat and charged out the back before he realized he was all but running to catch up.

Zoe rushed them both along so fast with her energetic enthusiasm for anything to do with ranch work that she fairly wore J.D. out. She fidgeted her way through his meeting with the hands to discuss what needed to be done that day and who would do it. She'd gone with him to check cattle, doctor a few, and herd three yearlings who'd got tangled in barbed wire to the headquarters for stitches and antibiotics. She helped him repair the section of fence that had caused the injuries, checked three of the windmills, and insisted they spray for wasps under the eaves of one of the smaller barns later. "To thwart temptation," she'd declared, jerking a thumb in the direction of the Everdine house to indicate it was Bobby's temptation she meant to thwart.

They were riding back to the house for the noon meal when Zoe told him about receiving a copy of the biography in the mail the day before. When she finished giving him a brief rundown, she looked over at him.

"On the whole, it's a pretty brutal book, but in addition to leaving the kids' names out, Casey was much nicer to me than I expected."

J.D. appeared to be thinking that over. Irritation darkened his features. "Nicer?"

"Well, sure, J.D. He didn't once mention the words self-destruct, overdose, or the Betty Ford Center," she joked.

J.D.'s gaze shot to hers. He saw her grin and frowned mightily. "Hellfire, Hollywood, take the sneaky viper to lunch. What the hell kind of nice is that? He invaded your privacy, tormented you with worry about the kids, and wrote things about your personal life without your permission. That book'll have the media on you like fuzz on a peach. But, just because he didn't mention suicide or the Betty Ford Center, you think he treated you nice?" J.D. gave a harsh bark of laughter.

"We're talking comparatively nice here, J.D.," she insisted. "Compared to what he could have written— more in the form of speculation about how I'll end up rather than anything particularly scandalous, I'll have you know—Casey managed to stick fairly close to the facts and not make me sound like a pitiful neurotic. I've handled the media lots of times. Now that they won't be targeting the kids, I won't worry much until I see if anyone shows up here."

J.D. faced forward and shook his head. "Are you ever going to be able to live without some author or reporter digging into your private life and trying to make money on a story about you?"

His dark gaze swung back to hers and Zoe was rocked by the grimness she saw there. But then, she'd known J.D. wasn't the type to tolerate notoriety in a potential mate.

"I don't need to have media attention to be happy, John Dalton. But because of Jason and Angela, there will always be that potential." She shrugged and looked ahead of them to the headquarters in the distance. "I'll just have to hope it doesn't get out of hand before people lose interest."

J.D. was silent for a time, and Zoe was, too. His silence worried her, so she decided to divert them both.

"So, have you thought about your plan?"

J.D. glanced her way. "What plan is that?"

Zoe gave him a stern look and scolded, "No wonder you're thirty-four and have no heirs to Hayes, John Dalton. I'm talking about your plan to find a wife and get an heir going."

J.D. gave a cranky sigh, but Zoe grinned mischievously. "I've heard men can still father children when they're in their seventies or eighties."

J.D.'s prickly "Oh you have?" made her grin widen.

"But other than serving themselves a last bit of male vanity, what's the point—aside from proving it's possible?" She gave a wave of her hand as she expanded on the subject with relish.

"The old geezer dies before the kid's out of diapers, and the kid's mom either raises him alone or hopes to find a new husband to help her raise the child. A waste—not to mention that in your case, it would also be a matter of someone other than a Hayes in charge of running the Hayes Ranch. And how would you know if your young wife would make a good choice with another husband? He might turn out to be a gold digger or a con man who'd pick Hayes clean, run it into the ground, or sell it to someone who'd divide it up. He'd abandon your wife, take the money, and your child would end up without a penny to his name, living in a big city somewhere in a cheap apartment, without a clue about what you'd meant him to have or the history behind the Hayes name."

Zoe reached over and gripped his thick wrist to give him an urgent shake. "Daylight's burnin', partner."

J.D.'s formidable expression cracked and the glint of reluctant humor in his dark eyes delighted her.

"Bull." His one-word opinion made Zoe giggle and pull her hand away.

"So don't listen to me, John Dalton. By the time this horrid little scenario plays itself out, we'll both be planted somewhere, and we'll never know."

With that, Zoe touched a heel to Brute. The bay moved into an easy canter that carried them ahead of J.D.'s

sorrel. J.D. didn't rush to catch up, letting her reach the
stable far ahead of him.

It was two o'clock by the time they got to town for their
appointment at the lawyer's office. They'd both cleaned
up and changed their clothes. J.D. had settled on a white
shirt and a newer pair of jeans, but Zoe had clearly
dressed to express a bit of her flamboyant taste.

J.D. had seen the huge, silver belt buckle and black
dress Stetson the day she'd arrived at Hayes, but the
lively, multicolored paisley blouse and pink jeans she
wore with them was a complete surprise. The red western
boots she had on drew out the reds in the blouse and
matched her red silk neckerchief. And yet Zoe looked
chic, refined, and every bit a socialite playing cowgirl
dress-up. He had a hard time keeping his eyes off her.

He didn't have a prayer. Common sense had been
pounding him with that prediction for hours now. As
he pulled into a parking space and switched off the
engine, J.D. felt his mood sour. He'd wanted to get close
to Zoe that whole day. He'd wanted to see if he could
engineer something that would put them both in a position to follow up on that kiss the other night on the
sofa. But Zoe, full of fun and teasing and a dozen little
hit-and-run touches, had kept a careful distance.

J.D. got out of the car and walked around it to open
her door for her. As she stepped out, he closed the door.
He took her elbow, doing his best to make the move
look casual rather than the necessity to touch her it suddenly was. When she pulled her arm from his gentle grip
to slip her hand through the crook of his arm in a subtly
possessive way, his heart was given another nudge.

Just walking next to Zoe made him feel awkward and
oversize, hopelessly earthbound. Zoe didn't just walk,

he noted for the umpteenth time. She floated, skipped and danced along, like a golden good fairy with gossamer wings, magic slippers and a shiny silver wand to grant wishes to the deserving. J.D. no longer objected to the whimsical notions that Zoe seemed to inspire. She was both the genuine article and a fake; a bright hunk of gold covered with sparkling pyrite. In most ways, she was a gleaming enigma to him and might always be. Ethereal, illusive, rare. Zoe Yahzoo was too special for a rough country man like him, too delicate for his harsh, blunt ways.

But he wanted her. During the short time she'd been on Hayes—perhaps from that very first day he'd met her at the fence when she'd given him that brazen smack on the knee—he'd become addicted to the fairy dust she'd sprinkled over his harsh, humorless life. He'd not realized how much he'd let himself settle for sweat, hard work and the subtle bleakness of solitude. Until Zoe.

But happily-ever-after with Zoe was a chancy prospect. It wasn't her background or celebrity or anything about her that made it so. It was him. He was a no-fuss, no-frills, square-toed man—well on his way to fossilhood, if Zoe's teasing that day was any indication. And even J.D. knew the good fairy never mated with the troll. As powerful as her magic was, Zoe would never turn him into a handsome prince with elegant manners, or refine him enough to fit easily into the high society part of her life.

As J.D. reached ahead of them and opened the office door, Zoe glanced up at him, her neon eyes as bright and deep as he'd ever seen them. Her megawatt smile warmed him like a shaft of hot sunlight. She didn't seem to see he was a troll. Or that he was troll enough to hope she wouldn't for a long time to come.

*   *   *

Zoe did her best to appear as sunny as usual. It upset her more than she wanted anyone to guess that selling her one third of Hayes back to J.D. would cut an important tie between them.

Lord, she didn't want to leave Hayes; she didn't care if she ever left Texas or set foot in California again. Yet despite making up for lost time with her family, she couldn't hang around indefinitely. Now that she would no longer be J.D.'s co-owner, she wasn't comfortable taking up space in his home as a mere houseguest.

Perhaps she'd overdone it that day, needling him about marriage and heirs to Hayes. It had been all she could do to keep from proposing marriage herself, but in the end, she'd chickened out. She would have been devastated if he'd refused her.

And now she regretted pushing him to consider marriage at all. She couldn't bear the idea that she might have got him thinking strongly about it, only to leave Texas and find out later that he'd taken her advice and married someone else.

Zoe managed to cover her glum thoughts well behind her smiles to the receptionist, then to J.D.'s lawyer, Mr. Blake. Her personal lawyer was already waiting on the phone line by the time they were seated in the inner office. Mr. Blake switched the call from California onto the speaker phone, and once the pleasantries were out of the way, he started passing them the first of the papers they were to sign.

J.D. began to scan the top page of the papers, but Zoe addressed a question to her attorney. "Bianca, do you have any ideas about who might have sent me a copy of the bio? There was no letter with it and no return address. Oh—and you can speak freely, unless it's something awful."

"I certainly do know, Zoe. I got a call from Mr. Casey not more than a half hour ago on that very subject. It came from him, and you should be getting a letter." Bianca gave a knowing chuckle. "It sounded to me as if he has a crush on you. He'll probably mention lunch. He wanted me to convey his offer to do a book on you, but only with your permission. Or so he claimed."

J.D. made a sound that was little more than a snarl.

Bianca heard. "What was that? You aren't in a barn, are you?"

Zoe laughed at her attorney's appalled tone. "No, Bianca. That was my soon-to-be-former co-owner, Mr. Hayes. He's quite formidable and opinionated, and I'm...quite taken with him," she finished quickly. She'd not been able to resist getting that in before she changed the subject. "Are these papers safe to sign?"

"Of course, but you need to read them through anyway," Bianca counseled, and Zoe made herself do so. The room went silent for several minutes. As she began signing her share of paperwork, Zoe was aware that J.D. was still only flipping through his own. By the time she finished signing, J.D. had stopped reading and was simply watching her. The intensity of his dark gaze suddenly made her breathless.

Her soft, "Is something wrong?" made him glance at his lawyer.

"Give us a minute, Blake," he said gruffly. The attorney looked surprised, but he spoke a quick, "Hayes wants a minute alone with your client," to Bianca before he pressed the button that would take the call off the speaker phone. He got up and exited the room.

J.D.'s dark gaze pierced hers and Zoe had to resist the strong urge to glance away. He looked every bit as formidable as she'd told Bianca a few minutes ago.

"Are you aware that you have a pretty scary look on your face, John Dalton?" she asked softly. The restlessness she felt made her get up to place her sheaf of papers on the big desk before she turned back to J.D. and sat on its front edge.

J.D.'s gaze had followed her every move, but now it took a slow journey from her eyes to the toes of her red boots, which were now just a hand span from the toes of his big black ones. Zoe suppressed a tingle when his dark eyes made an unhurried return trip to fix on hers.

"What were you getting at this morning, Hollywood?"

J.D.'s utter seriousness was intimidating. Her soft voice was a little squeaky as she asked, "You mean about your plan?"

When he didn't shake his head to that, she answered with a stiff little wave of her hand. "Oh, I was doing the usual, John Dalton." His gaze was relentless, prompting her to be more candid than she had the courage to be.

"Actually, I was teasing you, but..." she hesitated, "I think you know me well enough by now to know I sometimes have a bit of a hidden agenda when I do that."

J.D.'s hard expression eased slightly. "What do you suppose became of that hot little kiss the other night?"

Zoe's heart shot into a wild, tripping rhythm as she watched him slowly come to his feet to tower over her. He tossed his papers to her empty chair.

"It seemed to fizzle pretty quick, J.D.," she said, a half smile sneaking over her lips as he frowned. "For you it seemed to." She let her smile widen. J.D. smiled then, too, but it was faintly predatory.

"How about for you?" he questioned next. Zoe slowly eased off the desk and came to her feet.

"It was...pretty good," she admitted with playful reluctance. "Of course, now that I'm starting to remember a bit more of it, I seem to recall that it had a kind of a..." She paused, then snapped her fingers a couple of times as if trying to think of the right words. She brightened, then pointed up at him to declare, "A legendary, comes-along-once-in-a-lifetime sort of feel to it." She grinned impishly. "But I'd have to have another one like it to tell for sure. You know, something a bit more up to date to compare it to."

Her breath caught when he stepped toe-to-toe with her. It made her dizzy to look up so far and she automatically inched backward. J.D. moved with her until she was backed against the desk.

"Then let's do a comparison." J.D. swept her up so swiftly and kissed her that Zoe's smile was more squashed curve than pucker. Her arms came up and lashed around his neck as her red boots dangled well above the black shine of his. Zoe gave back every bit as good as she got, somehow managing to be both the conqueror and the vanquished as J.D. urged, demanded and coaxed her to a wild frenzy of sensation and profound emotion. He didn't ease his lips from hers until they were both struggling for breath.

Zoe pressed a few small kisses to the long creases on his cheek. She got out a breathless, "Have you...made any plans yet, John Dalton?"

"As a matter of fact," he rumbled, but his mouth found hers and he kissed her again until they needed to breathe.

"I'm in love with you, Zoe Yahzoo," he whispered hoarsely as he kept her crushed against him. His dark gaze blazed into hers. He brought up a trembling hand and ran a knuckle down her flushed cheek. "Stay with me, baby, please. Be my wife and have children with me.''

Zoe stared into his harsh face. The raw earnestness she saw on his proud, rugged features made her eyes sting. His dark eyes were gentle, and the contrast between his innate toughness and his equally impressive tenderness made her heart burst with profound affection. She pulled her arm from around his neck and placed her small palm on his hard jaw.

''I love you forever, John Dalton, but do you mean it? Are you sure?'' Her eyes were almost impossible to keep clear of tears. She placed a finger over his lips to keep him silent. The insecurities she'd struggled with her whole life were making themselves felt, and she couldn't ignore them.

''I can't change who I am, and I don't think I can change very many of the things that come with that. There will always be the potential for media attention that you might not appreciate. I will always be connected somehow to Hollywood. Wouldn't all that bother you?'' She slipped her finger from his lips.

J.D. opened his mouth to speak, but Zoe hastily put her finger back on his lips as other thoughts occurred to her. They tumbled out on a swift torrent of nervousness.

''I'm kinda flighty, John Dalton. I don't always go about things the way other people might, and I have some character flaws. Besides which, I'm headstrong, I'm used to doing what I please, and I'm way too silly sometimes. In spite of what Casey didn't write in his book, I have an occasional neurotic moment that might make you crazy, but...''

Her voice lowered to a shaky whisper. ''I love you dearly, John Dalton. I love it that you're tough, but you're always gentle with me. I love it that you have integrity and strong ideas and that you're down-to-earth. I love it that you're blunt, that you aren't afraid to sweat and swear and act the way you feel and say exactly what you mean. I love you forever and I want to have at least six of your heirs—'' She tapped her finger on his lips as she switched the subject back. ''But you've got to think seriously about what you're getting into with me.''

For all her attempts to let J.D. know exactly what he was getting, Zoe prayed he wouldn't think about any of her warnings too seriously.

''And then there's Jason and Angela,'' she added, and rolled her eyes. She didn't want to elaborate on them at all. Besides, she doubted they'd trifle with J.D. once they met him. He was probably one of the few people she'd ever known who was tough enough to blow them off like dandelion fuzz.

Zoe moved her finger, her worried little ''Okay, that's it,'' was followed by a small smile that trembled.

J.D. was watching her face, his dark eyes probing hers. ''That's it?'' he asked tersely.

Zoe nodded and took a quick breath. ''As much as I can think of while I'm rattled.''

J.D. grinned, the suddenness of it startling her. ''*I'm* naming our kids.''

Zoe's brow crinkled in a faint frown that was pure playacting as she felt love surge in her heart. ''Oh, you are? You think John Dalton, Jr., Nick, Victoria, Julia, Henry, Flip and Gomer are too bizarre for Hayes kids?''

His deep rumbling chuckle shook them both. ''No J.D., Jr. I won't have any son of mine nicknamed Junior. Henry is a middle name, Flip and Gomer are for horses. I love you, Zoe. Will you be my wife?''

Zoe couldn't help the happy tears that shot down her cheeks as she gave him a huge smile. "I'll always love you, J.D., with all my heart, and I'll be your wife." She hugged him tightly as she struggled to get control over her jubilant emotions. When she finally did, she kissed him, doing her best to express a part of the love she felt for him. It was a while before she reluctantly broke off the kiss and gave him a teary smile.

"Your Mr. Blake probably won't appreciate that we took over his office and left him waiting so long. Bianca hates being left on hold."

"They're getting paid for their time, Hollywood. They can wait," he said gruffly.

"Well, I don't think I can, J.D. Let's get these papers signed and find the place where they hand out marriage licenses. I want to get my ZY brand on your hide before you start having second thoughts."

J.D. chuckled and shook his head. "There won't be any second thoughts, Zoe, not for me. And I'm not going to sign any of Blake's papers."

"Why not?" Zoe had already signed hers. Had J.D. seen something in his copies that he didn't like or wanted to have changed?

"Because I like having a partner, Hollywood. I like having *you* for a partner. We can both pass Hayes on to our kids when the time comes."

Zoe brought a hand to his lean cheek, overcome again with emotion. "I know how much Hayes means to you."

He nodded. "So maybe you have a better idea of what you mean to me, Zoe. Let's get out of here. We can be married the minute it's legal, unless you'd like to wait for a big wedding."

"Any wedding at Hayes will be a big wedding, J.D.," Zoe declared. "Carmelita, Coley and Gus—everyone will have to come. And I have a family that will be there, and a father to give me away.'' The reminder sent a few more happy tears skittering down her cheeks. ''We can have the ceremony on the front porch. I'll get a really good photographer, I can get a caterer here in three days so Carmelita and Coley can relax—I've even got a really old white wedding gown I bought at a costume auction a year ago, I—''

J.D. halted the excited torrent with a kiss. When he finally released her and set her gently on her feet, Zoe swayed in weak-kneed happiness. In moments, he'd swept her from the office, tossed his lawyer a brusque, ''Deal's off,'' and hustled her out the front door of the law office into the Texas heat.

A group of reporters, flanked by a handful of photographers, charged up the sidewalk at them. It was then that J.D. noticed the cars and vans that now cluttered both sides of the small town street.

Zoe's panicked, ''Uh-oh, John Dalton, here it comes,'' and her anxious glance into his face to gauge his reaction made him press her tighter against his side and hurry them toward his car.

''Give them a big smile and tell them whatever you want, Hollywood.'' He answered her quick little ''You're sure?'' with a growling ''Yes.''

J.D. managed to open Zoe's door and get her shielded behind it before the reporters reached them. He escaped to the driver's side and got in to start the engine by the time the chorus of ''Miss Yahzoo!'' came to a crescendo.

He heard one bold lady's, ''What comment do you have about Dillon Casey's Sedgewick biography?'' as Zoe put her foot in the car and eased in to close the door. She pressed a button to lower the window partway, then held up a hand to halt the babble of questions that

followed. Her light touch on J.D.'s arm was a signal for
him to start the big car forward.

Zoe gave a laugh to go with the thousand-watt smile
she flashed them all. The click and whir of cameras
picked up pace. Two video cameras were aimed at an
angle through the wide windshield to film them both.
The cameras kept up as the car rolled forward.

"You know I can't comment," Zoe called to them,
and gave a playful shake of her head. She turned to smile
at the rugged, stern-faced man beside her who was taking
it all in with grim patience.

She didn't answer the next question, "Who's the
cowboy?" or the new frenzy for attention it stirred. J.D.
pulled the big car onto the street and sped away from
the swarm of reporters who chased after them on foot
for a half block.

Zoe took a nervous breath. "That's just a taste. If
they don't already know who you are or where the Hayes
Ranch is, they will very soon."

J.D. reached over and gripped her trembling hand.
He laced her small, slim fingers between his big ones
before he looked over at her. "Blake warned me there
were reporters in town snooping around before we came
in for our appointment. Jess and the men are moving
some of the cattle to the front pastures by the highway.
Once we're through the gate, wire goes up and we'll run
a few head of cattle in to graze along the ranch road.
Our biggest, nastiest bull will be in that bunch. I doubt
he'll give those reporters anything but second thoughts."
J.D.'s big smile made Zoe laugh.

"Lets get to the courthouse and see about that license," he said gruffly. Zoe smiled happily and gave his
big hand a squeeze.

*   *   *

Zoe Yahzoo became Mrs. John Dalton Hayes in a private ceremony on the big front porch of the Hayes ranch house. It took a bit of vigilance to keep the cattle assigned to the ranch drive from overrunning the tree-shaded festivities in the huge yard. J.D.'s biggest, nastiest bull, Bodacious, much preferred his assigned task near the wired-over front entrance to the ranch. Zoe reckoned it was the activity of the reporters themselves as they tried to find a way past the cattle that kept the surly bull's attention. The only helicopter that showed up was the one J.D. hired to ferry in a few guests. He'd also hired it to fly the two of them away once the reception was over and Zoe had tossed her bright bouquet.

They spent their honeymoon at a secluded cabin on a small lake in the Ozarks. J.D. learned his bride could bait a hook and catch fish. Zoe learned that her tough Texas rancher was even more thrilling in bed than he was out of it. They changed each other's lives.

So much so, that the dark-haired son they conceived before their first wedding anniversary was named John Dalton, Jr. The fact that no one dared call the boy Junior was because the boy's daddy was so formidable—and his adoring mother referred to the boy as Johnny D. Their second son, Nick's, middle name was Henry, but the next four children were all blue-eyed blondes: Victoria, Julia, Sarah and Theresa Jane, who could ride and rope as well as their brothers.

The vast Hayes Ranch had heirs aplenty, but the most impressive legacy Zoe and John Dalton left their children was a legacy of love, laughter and tender devotion. The precarious match between the good fairy and the troll was exactly right.

ℋarlequin ℛomance®

Coming Next Month
Four great books for Christmas—
all with a special mistletoe magic....

#3435 DEAREST MARY JANE Betty Neels
Mary Jane was a stay-at-home. She was hardly surprised when famous
surgeon Sir Thomas Latimer seemed to have fallen in love with her
glamorous model sister, Felicity. But Mary Jane didn't want Sir Thomas as
a brother-in-law—she wanted him as a husband! Would her Christmas
wish come true?

#3436 UNEXPECTED ENGAGEMENT Jessica Steele
Holding Out for a Hero
Love didn't play any part in Lysan Hadley's engagement. She liked her
fiancé, Noel, and marriage seemed a sensible solution. Then Lysan was
invited to spend the holidays with tycoon Dante Viveros. Lysan soon
learned that there was more to life than being practical—and even more,
she realized that she was marrying the wrong man!

#3437 A MISTLETOE MARRIAGE Jeanne Allan
Hitched!
Justin Valentine was a man who had everything...except a wife. She had
run out on him two years ago. But now Cait was back, and determined to
make this the best Christmas ever. She was no longer the spoilt little rich
girl she'd been when they'd married, and she was going to prove that she
would make the perfect rancher's wife!

#3438 ACCIDENTAL WIFE Day Leclaire
Fairytale Weddings—Book Two.
Harlequin Romance invites you to a wedding...
                              ...And it could be your own!
On one very special night, single people from all over America come
together in the hope of finding that special ingredient for a happy ever
after—their soul mate. The inspiration behind The Cinderella Ball is
imple—come single, leave wed. Which is exactly what happens to three
unsuspecting couples in Day Leclaire's great new trilogy....

Nikki Ashton has to convince her boss, her sister and a whole assortment
of relatives that she is happily married—ecstatic, in fact! Getting the
wedding ring is easy, so now all she needs is for Santa to bring her a
husband! Jonah Alexander seems perfect...if only he can handle ecstatic!

AVAILABLE THIS MONTH:

#3431 BRINGING UP BABIES
Emma Goldrick

#3432 THE COWBOY WANTS A WIFE!
Susan Fox

#3433 TEMPORARY HUSBAND
Day Leclaire

#3434 DREAM WEDDING
Helen Brooks

Harlequin Romance ®

brings you

Some men are worth waiting for!

We hope you've enjoyed our year of the bachelor—
with a different eligible man each month! They're
handsome, they're charming and, best of all,
they're single!

Watch for a very special hero in:

#3436 UNEXPECTED ENGAGEMENT
by Jessica Steele

Finding Mr. Right isn't always a problem—it's
holding on to him!

Available in December wherever
Harlequin books are sold.

Harlequin Romance ®

brings you

How the West was Wooed!

We hope you've enjoyed our year of romance, Western style, so far! Now, with Christmas just around the corner, we have one more special cowboy for you—and he's about to be lassoed under the mistletoe!

Watch for:

#3437 A MISTLETOE MARRIAGE
by Jeanne Allan

Available in December wherever Harlequin books are sold.

And, if you like your heroes tough, rugged and one-hundred-percent cowboy, we'd love to hear your thoughts on our Hitched! miniseries. Do write with your comments to:

The Editors
Harlequin Romance
Harlequin Enterprises Limited
225 Duncan Mill Road
Don Mills
Ontario
Canada M3B 3K9

Merry Christmas, Baby!

A romantic collection filled with the magic
of Christmas and the joy of children.

SUSAN WIGGS, Karen Young and
Bobby Hutchinson bring you Christmas wishes,
weddings and romance, in a charming
trio of stories that will warm up your
holiday season.

MERRY CHRISTMAS, BABY! also contains
Harlequin's special gift to you—a set of
FREE GIFT TAGS included in every book.

Brighten up your holiday season with
MERRY CHRISTMAS, BABY!

Available in November at
your favorite retail store.

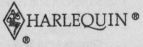